THE BEACHSIDE REUNION..

AINSLEY KEATON

CHAPTER 1

JESSICA

Jessica Bennett walked along the beach, feeling the cool morning air on her face. She tried hard not to think about her lover, her friend, her one and only solace in the world – OxyContin.

It had been over a week since she had her last pill. She had gotten past the physical sickness that inevitably followed after she quit cold turkey in the past – the nighttime sweats, this shaking, the tossing of her cookies after every meal. Now, she felt better physically, but there was still the void. The emptiness inside her heart had been aching for many years.

She knew what she had to do. She had lived in a house on the beach, an enormous mansion owned by her late grandfather, James Bloch. Unfortunately, her grandfather willed that house to somebody else. Her name was Ava Flynn, and, to Jessica's knowledge, Ava wasn't anybody to her grandfather. Jessica had no idea why her grandfather would've just given the house to a complete stranger, which meant she had to leave. She had to try to talk to Ava and see if she could possibly reclaim her life while staying in the house she loved so much.

At the moment, she was living in a van. She had to move around from one day to the next because there wasn't much parking on the island. She had been living in that van for the past year and a half, ever since she had to leave her home. Not that she faulted anybody for her life. Nobody was to blame but herself. But she had to take control, sooner or later. If she didn't, she would die. Literally.

With a heavy heart, she climbed the stairs to take her to the bluff walk. She would knock on Ava's door and beg her to take her in.

She had no other choice.

CHAPTER 2

ANDREW

Andrew Jameson was exhausted. There is no other word for it but exhausted. The past couple of years had been crazy, to say the least.

He never thought he could actually make music that people loved all over the world. He simply grew up around music, and when he was very young, something happened to him that was so tragic that he didn't speak for three years. He couldn't speak, but what he could do was write. He might've been only five years old when his world was ripped apart, but he was able to think of poems in his mind and write them out. He was a prodigy that way. And it saved his life because the poems were his only way of communicating with the world.

His uncle Frank was the one who encouraged him. When he was eight, Frank gave him a guitar and taught him how to read music. He also taught him all about the chords and their corresponding notes.

Frank got the guitar for him because his mom desperately wanted Andrew to communicate, and Frank thought maybe the guitar would help him come out of his shell. Nothing else was helping. At that time, nobody knew about his secret poems, so his mother wasn't aware he actually was communicating through his words. All she knew was all the therapy she was taking him to wasn't doing him a bit of good, and that, even though he did very well in school, his teachers couldn't get him to say a word in class, either.

About a year after he got his guitar, he learned how to write music. He was nine years old, he had been playing the guitar for a year, and he had learned from his uncle Frank all about chords, rhythm and tempo, melodies and harmonies, and notes. He could play the guitar and transcribe the notes he was playing.

And he finally spoke. He had written his first song, both the words and the melody, and he started singing to it. His mother heard him singing, and she rushed into his bedroom, crying hysterically.

"Oh my God, oh my God, I finally hear your beautiful voice. I was so afraid I would never hear that voice again."

When Andrew saw his mother's reaction to his singing his original song, his heart soared. But he still couldn't speak. He could only sing. So, that's what he did for the next year and a half. He sang instead of speaking. During that year and a half, he wrote over 100 songs about everything he was feeling in his heart. He wrote songs about kids at school who were bullying him, about his teachers who were constantly trying to get him to speak in class, and about his mother.

And he wrote song after song about his father, who was dead. Those were the songs that were the hardest for him to write, but they were also the most cathartic. He could finally unearth the trauma he'd experienced all those years ago. And, through this songwriting frenzy, he finally was able to speak for real.

So, it wasn't an exaggeration to say music literally saved his life. If he didn't have an outlet when he was very young,

THE BEACHSIDE REUNION..

he might not have been able to survive. The scars were just too deep. The memories were too haunting. His mother was a living embodiment of what happened to him, even though she was an innocent party, just like him. His mother was the most loving, caring person he knew. She didn't deserve what happened any more than he did.

His world became much brighter when he was able to finally speak and communicate with everybody around him. Kids stopped bullying him, teacher stopped pestering him, and he actually became quite popular in his middle school and high school. After all, girls love a guy with a guitar and a sensitive soul, and he had both of those things.

What he didn't expect was fame. But that's what happened to him after he graduated from high school. His uncle Frank knew a record producer in Los Angeles, and he sent this producer a demo of Andrew's songs. At that time, Andrew had a YouTube channel for several years, and his popularity was growing. His videos were seen by millions of people, and he had over half a million subscribers.

He never expected his YouTube channel to do anything for him. He simply had so many songs inside of him that were bursting to get out, and he was writing just about every day. He only wanted to do the YouTube channel because he wanted to share his thoughts with the world. He wanted to touch people through his music.

When the record producer got a hold of him, everything skyrocketed almost out of control. Before he knew it, he was touring the world. He was talking to the ladies on *The View*. He was featured in *Rolling Stone*. It was crazy how quickly everything happened. One moment, it seemed, he was making music in his bedroom and putting it on YouTube. The next, he was playing a sold-out show in Paris. Maybe it didn't happen that quickly, but it sure seemed like it did.

Now, he was 25 years old and bone tired. He was determined he would not be a flash in the pan. Yet, the record producer, Bill Kendall, was pressuring him to get his third album out quickly. "You can't give your audience a chance to forget about you. You have to get it done now!"

Getting a new album out wouldn't be a problem because Andrew had so many songs backlogged. Except he wanted to go in a different direction with his music. He had grown and changed and matured, and he no longer wanted to write dark songs. He wanted to embrace the light, and he wanted his next album to be about hope, love, and beauty.

So, he wanted to write all new songs for the new album. But he couldn't do that because he didn't do well with people breathing down his neck.

He needed to get far away from Los Angeles, as far away as possible. So, he talked to his mom and his best friend, Logan, to ask them for advice about where he should go to write his new album.

"Dude, here's what you should do," Logan said. "I'm gonna blindfold you, and then I'm going to give you a map of the United States. And then I want you to take a dart and stick it anywhere on that map. And wherever that dart lands, that's where you're going to go."

So that's what he did. He took a dart, and he put it on a map.

It landed on Nantucket. How odd, he thought. The dart landed on the one place that actually had a tie to him. It wasn't a good tie, not at all. It was where he grew up, at least where he lived until he was five.

He thought it was fate the dart landed there.

So that's where he was going to go.

CHAPTER 3

SAMANTHA

Samantha Flynn was at the end of her rope. Kicked out of her Brooklyn apartment because she couldn't make rent, she was now on Nantucket to beg her mom to give her a place to stay. But, she was extremely nervous about approaching her mom about it. She knew this was her mother's busy season with the inn, so she hoped against hope she'd be able to sweet-talk her mother out of a room in her home.

She called her sister Charlotte, who lived in Boston with her husband and infant daughter, Siobhan.

"Hey," she said.

"Hey yourself," Charlotte said. "What's going on?"

"I'm here," Samantha said.

"Here, where?"

"Nantucket. Drove to Hyannis, put my hoopdie car on the ferry, and here I am."

Samantha could almost hear Charlotte rolling her eyes. "And where have you been? Mom's been going through a lot these past couple of years, and you haven't been around."

"Hi, kettle, this is Charlotte. You're black! What have you done for her lately?"

"Shut up."

"Thought so." Samantha knew Charlotte never treated their mom very well. She didn't, either, but, unlike Charlotte, she never got on a high horse and accused her siblings of ignoring Ava. They were all three guilty of taking their mother for granted, and none of them could get the upper hand on the other in that regard.

"Off my case," Samantha said. "Where have you been?"

"I've been here. With my baby and my husband. I've been busy adulting, unlike you."

"Well, bully for you," Samantha said. "What, just because you accidentally got knocked up after lying to your husband about taking birth control, you think you have the right to be on a high horse, Charlotte?" She hated being grilled by her sister, who always tried to make her feel guilty for everything she did. As if Charlotte was such a perfect angel.

"No, not on a high horse. Just explaining why I haven't been around much. I know you haven't been around because you've been too busy drinking and meeting randos." Charlotte said.

Samantha wanted to have a comeback to that, but she really didn't. Charlotte was right - Samantha was a horrible daughter and much of the reason why was because she was too busy living her free-spirited life.

Of course, most of the time, the term "free-spirited" really meant too flaky to live. Most free-spirited people were just plain self-centered and irresponsible. Samantha was no exception to this, and she knew it.

"Well, I'm here now," Samantha said.

"And why are you there right now?" Charlotte asked.

Samantha rolled her eyes. "Oh, don't ask. I got kicked out of my apartment in New York because my stupid roommate

Grayson moved out here just out of the blue. Leaving me holding the bag. I don't know what gets into that boy."

Samantha was irritated beyond belief with Grayson. She had no idea what had gotten into him when he just announced a few weeks ago that he would live on Nantucket. It was something about him wanting to live close to a beach because it inspired his writing career.

However, she had no idea exactly why the beach would inspire his writing career. After all, he was a sci-fi fantasy writer, or he aspired to be. He wasn't yet published, but he always told her that it was just a matter of time before he set the world on fire like A.G. Riddle.

For her part, she dearly hoped Grayson was right about that. He was such a good dude. Except, of course, when he just upped and left on a wild hair, which caused a chain reaction that ended with her getting her butt kicked out of their Brooklyn tenement.

"Huh," Charlotte said. "So, you passing through or staying?"

"Staying," Samantha said. "Tired of the city, and I lost my job. Wasn't that why mom moved out here in the first place?"

"Not really. Mom moved out there because she had to. She inherited that gorgeous house, and she couldn't sell it or rent it out for five years. So, she would've been paying a shit-ton each year to keep that place up and get no benefits from it. But you knew all this. I'll bet you just decided to move out there on a wild hair."

"Nope. I decided to move out here because I'm tired of the city. Like I told you."

"Whatever."

What Sam didn't tell Charlotte was the *real* reason she decided to move to Nantucket. She decided she was going to snag herself a billionaire. Or, at the very minimum, a millionaire. After Grayson moved out to the island,

Samantha researched and found out the place was a playground for the rich. Her eyes popped out as she saw a silly little two-bedroom one-bathroom cracker box house was over a million dollars. It wasn't even on the beach, either. It was in the middle of some field.

She spent the entire miserable evening after Grayson left looking online at Nantucket homes. A house that sold for $59 million looked to her like an overgrown barn with an enormous lake in the back of it. Other mansions appealed to Samantha more, but she didn't think any of them were to her taste. But that didn't matter. She only saw that people were paying major scratch for Nantucket homes.

And she wanted to meet somebody who owned one of them.

The fact of the matter was, Samantha was tired. She was tired of working three jobs and not making ends meet. She worked as a butcher, a baker and a candlestick maker. Well, not actually those professions, but she made cupcakes for a Brooklyn bakery and waited tables for an Italian restaurant. In her spare time, such as it was, she delivered for Uber eats in her hoopdie 1996 RAV-4, which she called Priscilla because she was purple.

Well, she *was* purple. Now she was purple and silver because her paint job had long since worn off, leaving only patches of the purple paint still intact. Too late, Samantha found this was a problem with the 1996 RAV-4s - the paint was so cheap, it wore off in the sun.

She was running on a treadmill, and she really wanted off.

She was going to meet the billionaire of her dreams. They were out there, weren't they? Especially on Nantucket. She envisioned a hot young entrepreneur who showered her with kisses, gifts, and tons of money.

After all, every romance novel she'd read featured just

such a man in the middle of it. By the looks of things in the romance novel circuit, handsome young billionaires were a dime a dozen, and they were always looking for girls just like her to swoon over. Cinderella wasn't just a myth in her eyes.

Samantha had read books where innocent college students without a pot to piss in or a window to throw it out of snagged a handsome young billionaire. She read books where billionaires fell madly in love with homeless women. Books where bartenders and waitresses snagged a billionaire. Books where desperately poor girls auction off their virginity to help their sick mother or whatever, and the billionaire who bought them fell madly in love. She saw *Pretty Woman* about a bajillion times.

All these books were takes on the Cinderella myth, and Samantha knew Cinderella wasn't just a story. It was something to aspire to.

Samantha knew there was a good chance for her to snag a billionaire, too. After all, she was young and vivacious and cute. That was all she needed.

Of course, there was one huge problem with her plan. At the moment, she was flat broke, without a car or job. At the age of 24, she probably should've had something more going on in her life, but she simply didn't.

And she really didn't have a place to stay yet, which was another snag in her plan. Grayson had found a room living with a gay couple who had an inland house. So, needless to say, there was no room for her to live with him anymore.

Which left her mother.

She got to the beach and sat down on the sand. Samantha smelled the salty air, heard the seagulls and remembered how much she missed the beach. Her mother used to take her, Charlotte and Jackson to Montauk during the summertime on occasion. She looked forward to those visits to the beach like nothing else in her life.

"So, where are you now?" Charlotte asked.

"I'm at the beach. I'm going to go ask our mom for a room."

"Good luck with that. You know it's her busy season."

"I know that. Duh. Anyhow, I wanted to let you know that I'm on the island, and I'm here to stay."

"Where?"

"Where, what?"

"Where are you going to stay?"

Just then, Ava was on the beach. "I thought I saw you when I looked out my kitchen window. Samantha, what are you doing here?"

"Later, Char, mom's here." Samantha looked at her mother. "Hey, mom. I'm here!" She was stating the obvious, she knew, but she didn't know what else to say.

Ava gave Samantha a big hug. "My little butterfly daughter. How I've missed you." Ava had tears in her eyes.

"Missed you, too," Samantha said. "Mom."

"Well, come on and see my place. You haven't had the chance to see it yet."

"Sick," Samantha said.

Ava gave her a look. "You're sick? Do you need an aspirin or a Tums?"

Samantha shook her head. "No, mom, sick means cool. Don't be lame."

Mother and daughter walked to the house, and Samantha's jaw dropped. Her mother lived in a mansion.

"Mom. Your house is fire."

Ava gave Samantha a look. "What do you mean? There are fireplaces, but God forbid the whole place is on fire."

Samantha smiled. "Fire means awesome," Samantha said. "Actually, sick pretty much means awesome, too. But I think fire is even more awesome than sick."

Ava grinned as she opened up the door to her house. "I'm glad you like it."

Samantha followed Ava up the stairs and through a beautiful sunroom that led to an amazing deck that overlooked the ocean. She whistled softly as she saw how beautiful the space was.

A hot tub. Comfortable couches and chairs. Lights were strung up overhead. And when Samantha went to the edge of the deck, she could literally see the ocean.

"Wow, mom," Samantha said, feeling the ocean breeze on her face. "You can literally smell the water from here."

"That's true," Ava said. "It's my favorite part of the house." She smiled. "So, you just got here this morning, then?"

Samantha shook her head. "I got here yesterday afternoon," Samantha said. "But I ended up at The Chicken Box and met a guy."

Truth be told, she wasn't all that interested in the guy she'd met at The Chicken Box. His name was Dylan Hailey, and while he was fun and cute, he let Samantha crash at his pad, and she wasn't too impressed. He lived in a studio apartment in The Mariner House, and he worked from home as a web designer.

Thankfully, nothing happened between them because Dylan was so drunk that he passed out on his floor.

"The Chicken Box," Ava said. "A random guy." She shook her head. "Sam, you have to grow up."

Samantha rolled her eyes. "Do you get on Jackson's case for being a tool?"

"Jackson isn't a tool," Ava said. "And, yes, I know what a tool is. It's a jerk. Your brother isn't that."

"No, he's not. But he's waiting tables out in L.A. He didn't go to college. Do you get on his case about growing up?"

"No, I don't," her mother said. "Because Jackson is modeling, and he's getting acting parts. And he has a goal in mind. You don't seem to have any goals."

"I do have a goal."

"And your goal is?"

"To meet a rich guy out here and not think about lack of money ever again."

Ava shook her head. "Samantha, that isn't a good goal."

"It's not? Why not?"

"Because." Her mother took a deep breath and let it out. "That makes you a gold-digger. And that's a recipe for unhappiness."

"Why? Gran always told me it's just as easy to fall in love with a rich guy as a poor one."

"Maybe. But, Sam, here's the thing. If you're looking just at money, you'll settle."

"Settle, mom? Since when is marrying rich considered to be settling?"

"I mean, you'll settle for somebody who won't make you happy. If you're just looking at money, you'll overlook what makes a marriage work. Things like communication, having things in common, having common goals, and attraction. Being compatible. I worry you won't care about those things and that you'll only care about a man's fat wallet. Sam, you're going to miss the man who gives you butterflies."

"Says the woman whose second husband left her in the lurch."

Ava's face looked pained when Samantha said that, and Sam immediately felt horrible for poking her tender spot. Her mother meant well. She had her best interests at heart.

"Mom, I'm sorry. I didn't mean that."

"That's okay. You're right. I don't have the right to lecture anybody on what makes a good relationship because I obviously don't know myself. If I did know, I wouldn't have been left in the lurch by Christopher."

"I meant what I said. I'm sorry for saying that," Samantha said. "Anyhow, mom, I need a place to stay for a little while. So, what do you say? Can I stay here while I get on my feet?"

"I figured you'd hit me up," Ava said. "Your grandmother just left because she had to be back on the bench."

"Yes, I know. I figured I could just slide into her room, now that she's not staying there anymore."

Ava sighed. "Samantha, you can stay here, but you're going to have to earn your keep. I could certainly use some help around this place."

"What kind of help?" Samantha asked. "Mom, I'm going to be working a bakery job. Blue Moon Surfside."

"You already got a job? You said you just got here yesterday."

"I applied online. And, well, I have an interview today with Javier. He's the head guy over there, I guess."

"And what will you be doing over there?"

"I guess I'll be working in the café and bakery. Being a sandwich goddess or something like that, and baking their desserts, which I've gotten down."

Samantha didn't want to admit to her mother the *real* reason why she desperately wanted a job with Blue Moon Surfside. Aside from the fact that the place not only had a café and bakery where they served gourmet cupcakes, breakfast burritos, croissant sandwiches, açaí bowls, smoothies and bomb-diggity sandwiches, they also had a catering arm.

That meant she would be catering important events like weddings, bar mitzvahs and high-society functions. This would mean, in turn, she would be exposed to rich people. She knew she could meet her prince if she could doll herself up and work those functions.

And, most important to Samantha, they'd won awards for their wedding cakes. Sam secretly had a burning desire to be a cake designer. That was a dream she hadn't shared with anybody but Grayson.

She never admitted that she was not only addicted to bakery and cake shows - *The Great British Bake Off, Cake Boss, Ace of Cakes* and *Cake Masters* reruns were some of her favorites - but she also dreamed of being on a competition show. She knew she would be a great cake decorator if she were ever given a chance. She sketched ideas for cakes that she would like to make in her spare time, and she practiced making elaborate cakes in her kitchen. Grayson was a great guinea pig and had always helped her along.

When she found out Blue Moon Surfside was looking for somebody to work in their cafe, she knew she had to submit her application. She immediately got an interview because of her experience working 6 years at Vered's Pastry shop in Brooklyn. She got excited just thinking about all the weddings and social events she would be catering and all the eligible men she could meet at those functions.

She figured it would be two birds, one stone. She'd be able to work at events that would enable her to meet rich guys. And she'd hopefully get a chance to decorate wedding cakes. Maybe one day, she might be proud of her life instead of embarrassed about her hoopdie car, non-existent bank account and equally non-existent career.

Ava shook her head. "Sam, here's the thing. I have 8 rooms here I can rent out. I have to rent out all of my rooms if I'm going to make ends meet when the busy season is over. I put a lot of money into this place. I just don't know if I can afford to just give you a room."

Samantha rolled her eyes, but she understood. "Okay, mom, what you're saying is that I can't stay here."

"Yes, Sam, that's what I'm saying."

Well, that was great. Just fantastic. Now she was officially homeless. Thanks, Grayson.

"Mom, I don't have a Plan B."

"Dear, what happened to your apartment in Brooklyn?"

"Grayson moved out and moved out here, of all places. He's staying with some gay dudes on the North Shore. In a room. An individual room, mom. That means I can't crash with him."

"Okay," her mother said in a tone she used when Samantha was a little kid. It was maddening when her mom talked to her like that. As if she was just waiting for Samantha to throw a tantrum like a kid throwing a toy out of a crib. Which she used to do, according to Ava. "So, Grayson moved out, and?"

"And I couldn't pay the rent. Mom, I tried. You don't know how much I was working, trying to make rent. But I couldn't do it on my own. And, since Grayson moved out here, and you're also out here, I thought I'd join everybody. At this point, everyone I care about, besides Charlotte and Jackson, lives out here, so why not?"

Samantha watched her mother take a breath and felt annoyed. "Samantha, you have to stop being so impulsive," Ava said. "You could've found a different roommate in Brooklyn instead of just coming out here on a wing and a prayer."

"But mom, I *did* come out here on a wing and a prayer. And if you don't take me in, I'll be homeless. I mean, I guess I can move to Boston and crash with Charlotte if it comes to that. But I was really hoping it wouldn't come to that."

Samantha batted her blue eyes, hoping her mother would take pity on her. Surely Ava wasn't willing to see Samantha sleeping in a tent on a beach somewhere. Would she be?

"Okay," Ava finally said. "But you have to pull your weight around here. I'm going to need help running this place, and you can be that help."

Samantha didn't like the sound of that. "Am I going to have to clean toilets?"

"Of course," Ava said. "That's probably one of the most important things I'm going to need. That and making the beds, vacuuming the throw rugs, sweeping, mopping, dusting, doing the laundry for guests and helping out with serving. Also, cleaning the bathrooms -Windexing the mirrors, scrubbing the bathtubs and showers."

"Mom, I'm going to have to work at that bakery," Samantha said. She dearly hoped she could work at Blue Moon Surfside and her mother wasn't going to demand every minute of her time, which she probably would. Her mother tended to be absolutely anal about making sure everything was white-glove spotless.

"Samantha, what would you like me to do?" Ava asked her in a tone of voice that Samantha heard way too often from her mother. The tone of voice said that Ava was two seconds away from losing her temper. "Just give you a room? I'm charging people $400 a night, and I already have my rooms booked. Sam, you can't ask me to give you a room without my asking something from you."

"Well, I certainly can't pay $400 a night," Samantha said. "What would that be, mom, like $12,000 a month?"

"Yes, that's right. It would be around $12,000 a month. Or, you can work here and do what I ask you to do. It's your choice, Samantha, but what I can't do is just give you a room."

Was mom being a hard-ass? Or was she being a spoiled princess who just expected her mother to accommodate her?

She knew the latter explanation was right, but that didn't mean she had to like the situation.

"How many hours a week would you need me, mom?" Samantha asked.

"It would be a full-time job," Ava said. Then she shook her

head. "No, that wouldn't be fair. I'd say I'd need you about 20 hours a week at a minimum."

The job at the Blue Moon Surfside was full-time. They were going to need her to work the café and the catering end of it. She would be one of the cater waiters they would provide to all the summer events the place was booked for.

And, with any luck, she would at least lend a hand in creating the wedding cakes. She didn't know if she would get that chance, though. When she spoke with Javier over the phone, he said he had a girl named Cynthia making the wedding cakes.

So, basically, if she lived there, she would be back on the hamster wheel. Running and running and running and going exactly nowhere. Working 40 hours a week at the café and 20 hours a week at the 'Sconset Inn. She came to the island to get away from that grind.

And when would she get a chance to meet her Prince Charming with that kind of schedule?

She scratched her cheek nervously. She didn't know what to expect before she got here. She just figured she needed a place to stay, her mom was just handed this completely fire mansion with plenty of room for her, and that would be that. Ava would welcome her with open arms, and she'd be staying like a queen, in style, in one of Ava's many rooms.

"Mom, I'd love to work for you, but this bakery wants somebody full-time. And I think it'll be weird hours, too. A lot of early mornings and late nights. They serve breakfast there, starting at 7, so they might need me to open it up at 5:30, baking the bread and desserts. And when they cater events, they might need me to be a cater waiter."

Samantha clapped her hands as she thought about all the mansions she'd be able to visit when she became a cater waiter. Javier told her they already had several weddings lined up to cater and would be providing the cakes to most of these social events.

Ava finally sighed. "Samantha, I don't know what to tell you. You have to make a choice. Either help out around the inn or find another place to live."

"On Nantucket? Mom, do you know how expensive it is to live out here? There's like no apartment complexes, either. I mean, there's the Mariner House, but those places are like $3,000 a week. I checked."

Samantha started to feel a rising sense of panic. Her mother was right. She *was* too impulsive. She always went with her gut, her brain be damned. This wasn't the first time that she leaped well before she looked.

It would be the first time that leaping before looking absolutely bit her in the butt, though. Things always tended to smooth out whenever she made impulsive decisions before.

She was the girl who flew across the country to meet a dude in real life after only talking to him on the Internet. She was the girl who got a tramp stamp tattoo one night, and she was completely sober when she did it. She didn't want a tattoo before that day, but one morning, she woke up and knew she couldn't go another day before she got a Depeche Mode *Violator* rose on her lower back.

She was always doing things like that, too. She was lucky she wasn't ever murdered by a crazy serial killer when she swiped right on Tinder or Bumble.

Another example of her impulsiveness was when she decided to work at Vered's Pastry shop full-time instead of going to college. She was happy there and loved her job. But working there instead of going to college was an impulsive decision. She went through the whole college application process. Took her SATs and did well on them - she scored a 1172, which was good enough for her to get into some halfway decent colleges. Not Cornell, like Charlotte, but good enough for one of the state colleges.

But she saw the future, and it involved doing lots of math. She *hated* math of any kind. Really, she thought, who would ever use a quadratic equation in their lives? She couldn't think of anything more pointless to study. The only math she would ever need would be the math that involved measuring ingredients for a cake, and there was no solving for x involved in that.

While she knew she could get by with just taking a math class or two, she also knew that if she was going to major in anything, it would've been some kind of B.S. degree, with the B.S. *not* standing for Bachelor of Science. She probably would've studied underwater basket weaving or something like that and would've never gotten a job out of college.

Probably, she would've majored in drinking games and would've flunked out the first semester.

She just couldn't ask her mother to pay for schooling when she knew she wasn't serious about any of it. So, she knew she was doing the right thing when she got the job at Vered's when she was 18 years old.

Now she was 24 and about to be homeless, and she didn't think she was so smart in pursuing the bakery after all. Really, she should've buckled down and become a doctor or something like that. Not that she ever could've become a doctor, because math, but that seemed to be the only profession Sam knew about that would pay her what she needed to live.

And not just live but *live*. Enough money to take European river cruises and visit Middle Earth, also known as New Zealand. Enough money to buy a Tesla or another brand of electric car, because she hated contributing to global warming with her hoopdie cars. Enough money to buy an apartment with a rooftop garden and hot tub, like the one her mother lived in before she came to this place.

She sighed. She was just going to have to call Grayson and ask if the gay couple had enough room for her, too.

She hung her head. "Well, thanks, mom," Samantha said. "I just thought it wouldn't hurt to ask if you had something for me."

Ava gave Samantha a hug. "Sam, I'm sorry. I'm sure I'll have room for you after Labor Day when I'll have problems filling this place up. But I just can't spare a room right now."

Samantha took a deep breath. She was going to have to make something work out. If she didn't, what was she going to do?

She imagined maybe Jackson had room for her in Los Angeles. And that wouldn't be a bad idea because there were plenty of rich guys in Los Angeles for her, too.

But her fantasy was that she'd meet somebody there, on Nantucket. She pictured herself going on sailboats and yachts, drinking champagne and eating caviar with a handsome young billionaire who absolutely adored her.

She left the inn and called Grayson.

And, after she talked to Grayson, things didn't look quite so bleak after all.

CHAPTER 4

SAMANTHA

*A*fter her mother gave her the bum's rush, Samantha went to see Grayson. She would tell him about her horrible decision to quit her job and leave her apartment, all on faith that her mother would take pity and let her stay in one of her rooms.

Grayson never judged her when she made poor life decisions. Like when she met a random guy over the Internet. She swiped right on Bumble on a guy named Steve McNeil. She and Steve started texting and emailing back and forth, and, at some point, she found out he didn't live in New York City, but in San Francisco.

He wanted her to visit, so she did. Without even thinking about it. She asked Camilla, another girl who worked at the bakery, to cover for her, and she went out to San Francisco one weekend, spending all the money she had in her savings account to do so. She was dying to meet him because their emails and texts were flirty and fun, yet they also discussed important issues like politics and books they'd read.

Samantha thought Steve might be her dream guy and thought she could pop down to LA to see Jackson after meeting Steve, not realizing Los Angeles was an 8-hour drive from the City by the Bay.

When she met Steve, she realized it was all wrong. Not that he didn't resemble his picture, which was always a problem on Bumble or any other dating app. Sam couldn't count the number of times she met somebody IRL who looked nothing like their picture. One guy had apparently gained 100 pounds since he took his online picture, while another guy used a picture of a male model for his profile.

No, the problem with Steve was that there was zero chemistry. Even though their emails were thoughtful, fun and flirty, she found it difficult to converse with him. He kissed her that evening, and she felt revulsion.

Worst of all, she found out he didn't like dogs. Not that he was afraid of them or allergic to them. But he didn't like them.

Samantha had always had a policy not to date anybody who didn't like dogs. What kind of a person didn't like dogs? To Samantha, canines were one of the things that made life worth living, along with the music of Tori Amos and the television show *Downton Abbey*. Samantha was one of those girls who gross people out because she let dogs lick her right on the mouth. Whenever she saw a dog, she would lay down on the floor and let the mutt cover her face with doggy kisses, and that was one of her favorite things.

Samantha ended the weekend feeling dejected. She'd spent $1,500 on the trip to San Francisco, and that was with her staying in a fleabag hotel that stank of mold and had a filthy bathroom. Granted, San Francisco was a beautiful city. Steve thankfully told Samantha on the first night he wasn't interested, which left Sam to spend two days exploring the city on her own, so things weren't that dire.

Their decision to not see one another again was a godsend, really, because she loved walking around and admiring the Victorian homes. She walked all around the city, exploring China Town, Japan Town, The Pacific Heights and Haight-Ashbury, and was entertained by the sea lions crowding the docks on Pier 39. She rented a bike and rode across the Golden Gate Bridge into Sausalito and even biked over to where some enormous Redwood Trees shot hundreds of feet in the air.

So, the weekend wasn't a total bust, but Samantha regretted it just the same. She had to live on Ramen Noodles and Kraft Mac and Cheese for a few months after that trip, and every time she had to tell one of her girlfriends she couldn't meet up for drinks because she was broke, she cursed Steve's name.

But Grayson never said a word to her about her horrible judgment. He just teased her a little, as a big brother would do, but he certainly didn't lecture her. He even brought food home to her when he knew that she'd run out of groceries.

The problem was that Samantha made a lot of those bad decisions. She would get drunk at a bar and not have the money for a cab, and her Uber account was dry because she didn't have money in the bank to back up her debit card, and she'd ended up walking home at 2 AM, through rough neighborhoods. Drug dealers pestered her to buy from them as she walked past, and homeless guys begged her for money. One guy followed her for blocks, scaring her to death.

When she got home and told Grayson the next day about her journey home from the bar, he got angry. "You know if you're stuck, I'll come and get you. No matter the hour."

She knew that, but she didn't want to bother him.

"And if you would've been raped or mugged on the way home?" Grayson had demanded. "How do you think I would've felt? Really, Sam, you have to use your brains once in a great while."

However, Samantha continued to do dumb things, apparently not learning her lesson. How she managed to get through 24 years without getting an STD, an unwanted pregnancy, a DWI or having her body wash up in the East River was a miracle.

That was one of the reasons why she was anxious to become established on Nantucket. She saw the island as a safe place where she couldn't get into too much trouble. She knew it was only a matter of time before her bad decisions caught up with her, so it was time to stop making these poor choices.

She was tired of living on borrowed time, and she knew that moving to the island meant that she no longer was.

She found the house where Grayson was staying, a wood-shingled Cape Cod covered in roses, with a two-car garage. Grayson answered the door, and she followed him to his room, which was tiny and cramped.

"So, Grayson," Samantha said. "I guess I have to go back to Brooklyn. And hope to God I can find a place *tout de suite*. Oh, Grayson, I really made a mess of things."

He smiled. Grayson was really a cute guy, with floppy black hair, a strong Roman nose, and beautiful blue eyes. He was tall and fit and wore cool Elvis Costello glasses, black-rimmed and rectangular. His lips were pillowy, his teeth perfectly straight. He had a smile that lit up any room.

When she imagined herself as Nora, the heroine in her favorite book, *The Midnight Library*, she thought there was probably a life in one of the parallel universes where she and Grayson were married and had three kids. But in this world, in this universe, he was like her big brother. And, like a big brother, she prayed he could have a solution to her self-made problem.

"You might be in luck," Grayson said. "The guys I live with had a young couple move out of their granny flat. They asked me if I wanted to move in, but I couldn't afford it."

Samantha felt excited when Grayson told her this. "How much are they charging?" she asked.

"$2,000 a month," he said. "I'm only paying $1,000 a month for this room."

$2,000 a month. Could Samantha swing half that rent? Probably. That's what they were paying for their Brooklyn apartment. Her bakery job was advertised for $15 an hour, which she made in Brooklyn. Money was tight in Brooklyn, and it would continue to be so here.

She probably would get a second job waiting tables, which she did in Brooklyn to make ends meet. That is, until she found her rich guy to take care of her. After that happened, she would move into a mansion on one of the beaches.

"Do you think I can take a look at the granny flat?" Samantha asked. Suddenly, her situation didn't seem so dire.

"Sure," Grayson said. "I think Del might be home. He usually is. He works from home doing fundraising for a non-profit hospital. His husband Joe is a doctor who keeps odd hours."

The two of them went to a different part of the house that was apparently a sunroom. It had hardwood floors, colorful throw rugs, and the sliding-glass door looked out into a beautiful garden with hummingbird feeders. Butterflies and hummingbirds darted around the flowers and plants.

There was a desk in the corner and some extremely comfortable-looking couches and chairs. A middle-aged man with a slightly paunchy middle and long gray hair tied up in a man-bun was sitting at the computer, working.

He looked at Grayson and smiled. "Hey, Gray," he said. "Who's your friend?"

"Samantha," Grayson said.

"Samantha," Del said. "*The* Samantha?" He smiled at her. "Gray, you were right. She's a real cutie, isn't she?"

Sam looked at Grayson curiously. His face was turning bright red.

Samantha wondered how much this guy knew about her already. And she was a bit surprised that Grayson had been telling people about her.

Evidently, whatever the guy knew about her was positive, so that was a good thing for sure. At least the guy wasn't giving her the stink-eye and saying her name like it was a cuss word.

Del stood up and gave Samantha a hug, taking her aback just a bit. But she hugged him back because she liked friendly people.

"So, Sam, I can call you Sam, right?" Del asked. "Or do you prefer Samantha?"

"Sam's fine," Samantha said. "Most people call me Sam."

"Sam," Del said. "What brings you to our beautiful little island?"

"Uh, my mom lives here," she said. "She inherited this awesome place on Siasconset. She made it into a bed-and-breakfast. It's called the 'Sconset Inn. Maybe you've heard of it?"

"I have," Del said. "I've gotten notices on Facebook about that place, and I visited the website. It looks beautiful, and it's right on the water. Your mom should make some major bank on it."

Sam nodded her head. "Good, I'm glad you know about that place because it means the word's getting out."

"So, you're visiting, then?" Del asked.

"Actually, no," Samantha said. "I have a job opportunity out here." She suddenly felt embarrassed that said job opportunity was a $15 an hour job at a deli and bakery. She felt she should've accomplished much more in her 24 years and always felt apologetic that she wasn't working on something amazing.

"Oh? What kind of a job are you going for?" Del asked. "There's not much opportunity on this island unless you work from home like I do, or you want to go into the service industry."

"I have a job opportunity at the Blue Moon Surfside Bakery and Deli," Samantha said. "I'm going to be making wedding cakes." That was a white lie, but Samantha didn't want to admit that she would be working the deli and being a cater-waiter.

Somehow, being a wedding cake maker sounded prestigious to Samantha's ears. Wedding cake makers and designers were artists. They created the centerpiece of any elegant high-dollar wedding. The cakes at these exclusive weddings rightfully earned a lot of oohs and ahs, and many an Instagram page had been devoted to them.

But operating the counter at a deli and bakery sounded much less glamorous. Being a cater waiter sounded to Samantha a bit more prestigious than operating the deli counter, but it still didn't sound as impressive as being a wedding cake designer.

Del clapped his hands together delightedly. "Oh, a cake designer," he said. "I love watching shows about cake designers. Those cakes always look so yummy. But sugar is my Kryptonite, sadly. I love sugar, but it seems to despise me." He gestured to his slightly paunchy middle. "If I ever hope to see a six-pack again in my lifetime, I have to stay away from any white food."

Samantha smiled. "Don't be silly. You look great. And you only live once."

"Says the 24-year-old hotty with the 24-year-old metabolism. Missy, just you wait 20 years, then you'll be singing from a different song sheet. But more power to you. Eat that sugar and butter while you can and enjoy yourself. Do you have pictures of any cakes you've made?"

Samantha looked at Grayson, knowing she'd been caught in her lie. If she were a wedding-cake decorator at a prestigious bakery like Blue Moon, she would obviously have a body of work and experience. She probably would have an Instagram page devoted to her creations.

The truth was, the only cakes she'd ever designed were on paper. While she'd drawn many cakes when she would daydream about being a cake designer, she'd never gotten the chance to create an actual cake.

"Samantha has beautiful cake designs," Grayson said. "I've seen them. But I don't think she has any pictures. Do you, Sam?" Grayson asked.

Samantha was halfway tempted to download some pictures of other cakes off the Internet and try to pass them off as her own, just so she could make this Del think she really was what she said she was. She had no idea why it was important that the people she met thought she was somebody accomplished.

It was just her insecurities rearing their ugly heads again. *Why can't I just love who I am?* Samantha thought. If only she could love the person she was, she'd be so much happier.

As she stood in front of Del, she thought again about how she would change her life. When she was the wife of a billionaire, she would never have to apologize for being a loser. Everybody would just assume she was a woman of substance. Nobody ever questioned billionaires' wives and inadvertently made them feel embarrassed.

Del nodded his head. "Well, I'd love to see your work sometime. Again, I can't actually eat any of your creations, but I can look at them and drool, can't I?"

Sam smiled and nodded. "That's what cake decoration is all about. Creating the fantasy. You get to dream up such beauty and bring it to life. And then you get to eat it, and nothing is more amazing."

Del swiveled in his chair, a grin dancing on his weathered-yet-handsome face. "Tell me, Sam, what are your favorite flavors?"

Without missing a beat, Samantha said, "Blood orange and dark chocolate. Or any kind of fruit combined with rich dark chocolate. I mean, a cake with Chambord, raspberry preserves and ganache is absolutely heaven on earth. Or lemon mousse with raspberry puree. Maybe Grand Marnier or some other liqueur with Red Velvet cake. But you know, Bananas Foster with caramel, rum and cinnamon would be amazing, too."

Samantha's mouth started watering as she talked about the cake flavors that were a part of her waking dreams. She'd not only spent hours watching baking shows of all types, but she also spent countless hours looking on Instagram for inspiration.

Del nodded his head. "Fruit and chocolate, yes! Oh, it's been so long since I've had a really good piece of dark chocolate. What is your favorite kind of chocolate?"

"I like this brand called Endorfin. It has coffee and cardamom in it, but it's really subtle, so it just brings something interesting to the chocolate. But, really, I just like dark chocolate anything. And I do love me some buttercream flowers."

Samantha rolled her eyes in pleasure as she thought about the delicious little flowers she'd tasted on other people's cakes, as well as the flowers she made for Grayson.

"Mmmm," Del said. "Well, that settles it. You need to leave and never come back to my house, ever again. I've been off sugar for a year, and here you come, like a Jezebel, getting me to thinking about the white devil all over again."

Then he smiled. "I'm joking, of course. I'm delighted to

meet you, and, really, you can come and see Grayson whenever you like."

Samantha looked at Grayson meaningfully with an expression that said *go on, ask him about the granny flat.*

"Actually, I'd like Samantha to be here quite a lot," Grayson said. "As in, we'd like to look at the granny flat and maybe move in."

Del looked at Grayson and Samantha. "Oh, really? Well, I'm sorry, there's a morality clause. I can't rent to sinful cohabiters." Then he grinned. "Again, joking. Samantha, I'd love to have you. Can you pass a credit check?"

Samantha drew a breath. The answer to that would be a big, fat "no." Unfortunately, she'd gotten in some trouble with credit cards when she was 18 and had to declare bankruptcy. That, combined with her recent eviction from the Brooklyn apartment, would sink her.

"Actually..." Samantha said. "I have to be honest. My credit isn't the best. I had a recent eviction and a bankruptcy when I was 18."

Del shrugged his shoulders. "Thanks for being honest. I'll let you move in anyway, but don't tell Joe you have crappy credit. He would kill me. We've had renters run out on us, and Joe's told me we can only have A+ renters. But I like you, Samantha. You have good energy. I'll bet you're a Sagittarius."

Samantha cocked her head. "I am, actually. My birthday is December 10. I'm one of three."

"One of three?" Del asked.

"Yeah. I'm a triplet. My sister Charlotte isn't like me. She's very serious and sometimes very mean. My triplet brother Jackson is very chill. But of the three of us, I'm probably the most free-spirited."

When Samantha said she was free-spirited, she really meant she was impulsive, made terrible life choices, and couldn't seem to settle down. But the term "free-spirited" sounded so much better.

Del clapped his hands. "Yes, a fellow fire sign! I'm a Leo. Born August 7. I love Sagittariuses. They're always so fun and free. As a Leo, I have a big heart, and I'm very ambitious, and I'll do anything for a friend."

Samantha smiled. She really liked this Del.

"So, I really can move in?" she asked.

"Sure. I mean, I hope you can make rent with Grayson here to help out, but if you can't, it's no big deal. I mean, I'll have to kick you out, of course, but the world won't come to an end." Then he smiled a devilish smile. "But I have a feeling, pretty little Samantha, you'll do just fine. I get the feeling you're a girl on the move. I don't know. I think you have some great things ahead of you."

Samantha's heart soared. "Oh my God, thank you so much!" She excitedly hugged Del, who laughed heartily.

"What are you thanking me for? I'm not doing you a favor. You're going to have to come up with half the $2,000 rent, girly. You're doing me a favor, really. I mean, I'm not going to have to do the dreadful process of trying to find somebody to live in that granny flat. Now, let's go and take a look at the place."

Samantha and Grayson followed Del across the courtyard to a small house in the back of the larger house. The granny flat looked, from the outside, like a smaller version of Del and Joe's house. It was a tiny Cape Cod with wood shingles and its own little porch.

Del turned the lock, and Samantha took a look around. It was cute inside, albeit small. It had its own kitchen, with granite countertops and new appliances. The floors were new hardwood, and it had two tiny bedrooms. The place was probably less than 600 square feet, which was about the size of their Brooklyn apartment.

She knew when she saw the place she'd found her home. She loved Del and was excited to be renting from him. And she and Grayson made really good roommates. After all, they'd lived together for 6 years, ever since she'd found him on Craigslist when she was moving out of her mom's place and looking at places in Brooklyn.

****

Later that day, after Samantha signed a lease, Del told her she could stay there right away. There wasn't any furniture in the place yet, but there was an air mattress. Samantha took him up on it and then panicked just a little. She had no furniture. She'd abandoned all her furniture in her Brooklyn apartment.

She was going to have to do things ass-backward - she was going to have to get the job at Blue Moon, and she would have to work Door Dash, which would pay her money right away, and then she would get furniture. After a few shifts with Door Dash, she'd have enough money to buy a bed and dresser off Craig's List and a decent mattress. She and Grayson would have to go in on the rest. They would be able to get some hand-me-down sofas, chairs, a dining room set and a few coffee and end tables.

But, for now, she would have to sleep on the air mattress.

It didn't matter. She'd landed on her feet and found a home. For that reason, that air mattress brought her more comfort than anything ever could.

CHAPTER 5

AVA

One day, early in the morning, Ava got a new guest. Her name was Jessica Bennett, and the way she came to the inn was something that was entirely unexpected.

She appeared on the porch, a tiny little thing in a jean jacket, ripped up pants, and shoes that had seen better days, to say the least. She stood there and then lifted her head. "My name is Jessica Bennett," she began.

When Jessica said her name, Ava put her hand to her heart. She had been bracing herself for this moment for as long as she could remember. Well, as long as she'd been in the house and Deacon had told her that Jessica had been living there and had to leave to make room for her. Ava always wondered what happened to Jessica, but she tried to put it out of her mind. Now, here the young lady was, and Ava wasn't quite ready for her.

Jessica looked uncomfortable. She was standing there, right on the threshold, her hands clasped in front of her, her shoulders slumped. She didn't look Ava in the eye. It was if she couldn't.

As Ava looked at her, she could feel the emotional issues

this girl was carrying with her. It was palpable. She suddenly wanted to wrap this girl in her arms and become a mother figure for her. There was just something about how she looked that brought out Ava's maternal instincts.

"Come in, come in," Ava said to the young woman. "Uh, let's go up to the deck, shall we? We can talk up there in private."

Jessica and Ava went out to the deck. It was early in the morning, so her guests had not yet come up to hang out on this terrace. So, everything was quiet up there. The beach was silent below. Only the waves and the shrieking of seagulls could be heard in the distance.

"Have a seat," Ava said with a smile. She could still feel that this girl next to her, this beautiful girl, was distraught. "Can I get you anything? A bottle of Perrier? Some snacks?" Ava didn't know quite what to say to this young lady. She knew she was babbling, but she couldn't really help herself. Suddenly, she realized that she wanted Willow to be there. Willow would be able to draw this Jessica out.

Jessica shook her head. "I'm sorry to be barging in on you like this." She hung her head and started to cry. "I'm so sorry. I'm not your problem. It's just I have no place else to go, nowhere to turn. And I really need to get my life on track. And to do that, I need a safe place to land."

Ava put her hand on Jessica's hand. "What can I do to help you?"

Jessica took a deep breath. "I've had a problem for the past few years. I have an addiction to OxyContin. And it's gotten so out of hand that I can't stay with my parents. Well, I can't stay with my father and his wife. My mother is dead. She died when I was a very young girl."

Ava's heart went out to her. She knew what it was like to lose a parent at a very young age. Ava's own father had died when she was only six, but she recently found out the man she always thought was her father really wasn't. That all got sorted out with her mother, and things were okay between her and her mother, Colleen. But, for a while there, she thought that would never happen.

Ava felt guilty that Jessica had to move out of this house to make way for her. How was that fair? It wasn't. And she had intended to get in touch with this girl, but she got so busy with everything that had been going on in her life, so she just didn't get around to it. Now, here she was.

It was just as Ava had feared – a part of her knew Jessica was a troubled soul because of how Deacon described her. The fact she now had her suspicions confirmed relieved her in a way. At least she didn't have to hold her breath in fear anymore of confronting the girl.

"What kind of help can I give you?" She didn't want to offer her money because she feared Jessica would just blow it on drugs. Perhaps she could pay for her to check into rehab, although she didn't have the liquidity to check her into an outstanding facility. From what she understood, rehab, or at least a good rehab, cost a pretty penny - up to $70,000 a month. "I understand your bewilderment. Believe me, I know what it's like to feel you don't have any options. So, I'd love to help you."

Jessica visibly drew a breath and let it out. She was shaking just a little bit as if she was cold. And maybe she was.

Jessica sat in her chair and said nothing. It was July, but it was in the morning, so it was probably around 60 degrees. So it was entirely possible she was cold. Ava felt comfortable, but she wasn't dealing with withdrawal as this girl obviously was.

"Just a second," Ava said. And then she got up and went into the sunroom, which connected to the deck. She had an armoire there that had various blankets folded neatly on shelves. She went back outside and offered Jessica a thick fleece chocolate-colored blanket.

Jessica gratefully took it and wrapped it around her. "Thank you." Her voice was soft, shaky. It occurred to Ava that her voice was as shaky as her limbs were. Ava wondered if the girl was coming down, or maybe she was just actively high. She didn't know the signs. She'd been lucky that none of her children had ever struggled with drugs.

Jessica finally sighed. "I don't want to ask this of you. Believe me, as I was down at the beach below, walking up and down it all night long, I struggled with what I was going to ask you. But I need a place to stay. I don't have any money anymore. I blew that with my stupidity and my addiction. And I don't have a job." She hung her head. "Believe it or not, I haven't always been like this. I was respectable. I was going to be working on my master's in marine biology at BU." She swallowed hard and took a drink of her Perrier. "That was three years ago. "

Ava looked at the girl, wondering how old she was. Ava thought maybe she was in her early 20s, but perhaps she was older than she thought. "What happened in those three years?"

She bit her lower lip. "I had an accident. It was something foolish on my part. I was skiing in Vail. I'm a pretty good skier, but my friend decided she wanted to go off-trail. You know, where there are a lot of trees, and it's super steep. I didn't want to go off-trail, but I didn't want to say no. I didn't want to look like a chicken in front of this girl. I wanted to impress her. I know it's hard to explain, but she was somebody who was out of my league. And I don't mean that in a lesbian type of way, but in a friendship type of way. She was somebody who was in a top sorority house at BU, the popular girl, the unattainable girl I always wished I could be and never could."

Ava knew that feeling very well. She never liked to admit it about herself, but she did the same thing. She remembered when she was in school herself and how badly she wanted to be friends with some of the girls in the "good" sorority houses. They never accepted her because she wasn't in a house herself, but that was all she ever wanted.

If she put herself into the *Breakfast Club* characters, she always wanted to be Claire, but she was Allison instead. She never quite fit in. Not that she would deliberately spend an entire Saturday in detention because she had nothing better to do, but she could identify with the feeling of being an outcast. So, she could understand why this girl would try to desperately impress someone she felt was better than her. Whether or not the person was better than her was debatable, of course. In reality, being an Allison was probably better than being a Claire.

"Anyhow, I didn't want to not do something in front of this girl. I didn't want to admit I was afraid. So, I followed her off-trail. And, of course, I wrecked. I hit a tree as we skied downhill. I ended up in the hospital for a month. I couldn't go back to school, and that was the least of my problems. My big problem was that I was on painkillers for months. And, for the first time in my life, I started to feel good about myself. When I was on OxyContin, I had this kind of euphoria I had never experienced before. My whole life, I felt I just was a nobody. But when I was high, I was somebody. So that's what it was, more than the fact that the OxyContin killed the physical pain. It killed the mental pain."

Ava put her hand on Jessica's hand. "How did you get along?"

She shrugged. "I didn't. I went to see my granddad. I was desperate. I needed a place to stay. He was kind enough to let me live in this house. For some reason, he had this house as one of his properties, but it wasn't occupied. I guess he just didn't bother to find somebody to rent it out to. I don't know. So, I lived here for several years. The place was so huge that I couldn't afford to heat it or cool it, so I just lived upstairs in the sunroom. And, to be honest with you, I don't think my granddad did me any favors in the end because he enabled me. The only thing I did when living here was get high."

Ava wondered how she could pay any expenses if she didn't work during that time. But Jessica read her mind.

"Oh, granddad also gave me a small stipend to live on. $500 a month. But I had like no expenses, aside from the OxyContin. And I was also on food assistance, so I could eat. Not that I ever wanted to eat, but I got by. Then, when my granddad died, I had to leave. So, now, here I am. I've got nowhere else to go."

Ava took a deep breath. She knew what the easy answer was. She didn't owe this girl anything, legally at least. She could have just turned her out and told her she didn't want to help her. That's what she would've done if she didn't have a heart. Yet, she did have a heart. She didn't know exactly what she should do for this girl, but she knew she had to do something.

"Well, as you know, this is a large house. Lots of bedrooms. Do you have anybody you could turn to to get you into rehab? If you can do rehab, you are welcome to stay here after you get out."

Even as she said those words, she wondered if that was the right solution. She was so busy running the place. When would she have time to care for a drug-addicted woman? However, just like with many things in her life, she didn't think before she spoke. All she knew was this slight, beautiful young woman with the haunted eyes needed her help.

She nodded her head slightly. "No. I don't have the money for rehab. I was hoping I could start going to a 12-step class.

That's free, of course. I know taking me in would be a considerable risk, but you have to understand, I'm ready to walk away from the drugs. I've never been so ready for anything in my life."

Ava wondered about this girl's family. "Do you have any parents, any siblings, aunts, uncles?"

"Yes. But I burned my bridges with them. Did you ever see the movie *Less Than Zero?*"

Of course, Ava had seen that movie. That was one of the films in college that was required viewing for her and her friends. "Yes."

"Well, you know the scene where Julian goes back to Clay's father? He just wanted to crawl back home, but Clay's father didn't want him to? I believe the father was going to have him arrested for trespassing when he came to the house. I had a scene like that with my father. He doesn't trust me. My step-mother would like me to come home and stay with them, but my father has said no. He doesn't even care if I'm on the streets. Not that I blame him. I was such a good girl for so long. For 22 years, I was a straight-A student. Never had any problems, never got into any trouble. Then, when I got hurt, it all just went to hell."

"Are you on anything else? Other than OxyContin?"

She shook her head. "No. That's the only thing I'm on. I guess I'm lucky, if you want to call it that, that I have a supplier. When I say I'm lucky, I mean I haven't had to resort to taking street drugs. I have friends who had to turn to heroin because they could no longer get their OxyContin. It's cheaper, it has the same effects, and it's easier to find. But I found a supplier early on, and I treated this guy like gold."

"Okay." Ava wrung her hands as she sat next to Jessica. She didn't know what would happen next, but she had a good feeling that this girl was going to take her up on her offer to stay there in the house. From what the girl was saying, Ava was pretty clear that she didn't have anybody.

Jessica started to cry. "God, I didn't want to do this to you. I didn't. But I can't tell you how close I came to walking out into the ocean last night. Like in the Judy Garland or the Janet Gaynor version of *A Star Is Born*. Fredric March or James Mason just walking into the sea. That's what I wanted to do. But I figured I'd try one last thing - to ask you if you could take me in, and I could go to meetings as often as possible and do whatever I have to do to get off drugs."

Ava thought she should probably run her plan to bring Jessica into the house with somebody, but she didn't quite know who. After all, she was the boss of this place. She didn't need to get permission from anybody to do it. Granted, it probably would have been prudent for her to speak to Quinn, Hallie, Sarah or even Deacon and get their input. But Ava had to go with her gut.

"Can you get a job? Or can you do something around here? How are you with cooking?"

Jessica swallowed hard. "I'll do anything you need me to do. I can wait tables, chop vegetables, clean the bathrooms. Or just clean the house every day. Are you doing laundry service for your guests? I could do that. Just put me to work, doing anything. You don't have to pay me, of course. Just having me here would be more than enough payment."

Ava thought about all the work needed around the house and knew she probably could use an all-around girl to help out with things. The thought of having somebody to help out appealed.

Ava continued to wring her hands. It would be a considerable risk having this girl under her roof. She really should've at least spoken with Jessica's father to find out exactly why he didn't want her to come home and live with him and her mother. In *Less Than Zero,* Julian couldn't go home because he had a severe drug problem. He stole from his family and turned tricks to feed his habit. And that's what addicts did. They stole, they cheated, they lied. They did whatever they needed to do to get the money to feed their habit.

Ava finally sighed. "Let me find you a room where you could stay. I hope you don't mind that I want to reserve the rooms facing the beach for my paying customers. However, I have plenty of rooms facing the street that you can be in."

Jessica finally smiled for the first time. "You can find a closet for me, and that would be good. I don't care. I just need a roof over my head and a safe place to stay. And, as I said, I'll do anything around this house to earn my keep. If I don't, if I fall down, if I don't do everything you tell me to do, you can kick me out. I'll even drop for you anytime you want me to. Just give me random drug tests. I'll do them." Tears came to her eyes. "I can't tell you how much this means to me. You don't even know me, but you're willing to take a chance. That speaks a lot about your character."

Ava thought about her ex-husband, Christopher. Christopher had an addiction problem, just like this girl. His addiction took the form of gambling, not drugs, but it was an addiction all the same. It caused him to steal $1 million from her and leave her in the lurch. And, as much as Ava wanted to hate him every day of her life, she just couldn't. She only saw him as being sick, just like this girl. She couldn't save him, mainly because she didn't know he had a problem until it was too late.

She might not have been able to save Christopher, but she could maybe save this girl.

"Well, do you have any things? Clothes, books, anything like that?"

Jessica shook her head. "I've been living on the streets for months, ever since I've been turned out of this house, so no. I have nothing but the clothes on my back. Unless you want to count the cans and bottles I picked up on the beach." Then she chuckled a little. "Just kidding. I mean, I've picked up a lot of cans and bottles in my time for money, but I took them in a couple of days ago."

"Okay, then. Why don't we go and look at the rooms and I'll decide which one I'll give you for now? My hope for you is you can get off the drugs, and stay off the drugs, and try to get back into school at some point."

Ava suddenly realized she would look at this girl as a project. Much like the project she had just finished in renovating her house. Granted, she would have another project, which was the running of the bed and breakfast. But, with any luck, this girl could help out with that.

Ava and Jessica then went into the house, and they chose a bedroom that faced the street. Like all the other bedrooms, this room had its own balcony and fireplace and bathroom. Jessica whistled softly as she looked at the room. "You've done a great job with this place, you know. I mean, when I lived here, these rooms weren't half as beautiful as they are now."

Then Jessica hugged herself as she floated around the room. "I can't tell you how good this will feel to have a bed to sleep in tonight. My own bed, my own fireplace, my own balcony, my own bathroom." She examined the lilac candles and brilliant pink and white orchids and admired the paintings on the walls. Charlotte had helped Ava pick out all the artwork for all the bedrooms and all the other living spaces in the house. The paintings were, by and large, not particularly masculine or feminine.

In this bedroom, the central painting was of some women and children by the sea, all wearing wooden shoes as if they were in Holland during some long-ago time. Charlotte had explained that an artist named John Sargent, who lived during the 1800s, painted the picture, which depicted fishing peasants on the coast of Brittany, France. Ava didn't know much about art, not like her daughter did. She only knew what she liked and what drew her in. In this case, there was just something about the scene that spoke to her when she first found this painting in a yard sale. It spoke to her somehow, so she brought it home and framed it.

By the look on Jessica's face, she felt the same way about the painting. She was staring at the painting as if she was trying to crawl into the scene herself. She touched it lightly and then looked at Ava with tears in her eyes.

"What do you know about this painting?" she asked Ava.

Ava just shrugged her shoulders. "I don't know. My daughter, she's the art history major. She's the one who could tell you everything about every artist you might admire. I only know what I like, and sometimes I can't explain why I like a certain painting. It's just that some things speak to me and other things don't. In this case, I found it at a yard sale. And, I don't know, it just spoke to me."

Jessica nodded her head. "I guess I like this because it reminds me of the sea. As I told you, I was going to be working on my master's in marine biology when I got hurt. I grew up by the water, both here and in L.A, where I moved where I was young. Surfing, sailing, kayaking, swimming. Just always in the water. So, like you, I like paintings that remind me of water and the beach and the ocean."

Ava smiled. "Well, what can I say? I guess you'll be living in the right house if you love the ocean so much. You're just about the opposite of my daughter Charlotte. She hates the beach, but her husband is like you - he loves it. I'm probably in between my daughter, who wouldn't set foot on the beach unless she had to, and my son-in-law, who could probably go to the beach every day if he had his choice. I like the beach, but I have no desire to be down there every day. I do love the sound of the waves, though. That's why the deck of my house is my favorite place to be."

Ava, for some reason, felt guilty for calling this place "her house." At least, in front of Jessica, who Ava secretly felt the house belonged to. If Ava were to be honest with herself, she would admit that the main reason why she so readily consented to Jessica staying with her was that Ava thought, in her heart, that Jessica belonged there. She certainly didn't belong on the street, drug problem or no.

Jessica sat down on the bed and nodded her head. "I'm going to have to get some things. You know, little things like a toothbrush, deodorant, shampoo, conditioner, and clothes. I have a little bit of money, because, like I said earlier, I collected a lot of cans and bottles and took them in. So I have about 100 bucks." And then she laughed a little. "If you want to imagine how many cans and bottles it takes to add up to 100 bucks, all I have to say is it took me weeks to gather that much together. You're already doing so much for me, so I hate to ask you this, but I was wondering if you could take me to the store sometime soon?"

"Of course," Ava said to her. "Why don't we talk about you maybe earning a small salary here, in addition to room and board? I don't know. I'll have to crunch some numbers, figure out the value of your labor, and determine what would be fair. Of course, I'll be considering that you'll also be eating your meals here in addition to your room and board. But, I want to be fair to you, too. I suppose you're going to be doing chores around this house, such as the guest's laundry and washing dishes and cleaning bathrooms and chopping vegetables, or whatever I might need. In that case, you'll be entitled to a small salary in addition to room and board and food. I guess I say this because I think you're probably going to want to save up to buy a car."

Jessica nodded her head. "Yes. I liked what you said

earlier about my ultimate goal: to get back to school. That's my goal. To get my life back on track. I don't know how to do that, except I know that will involve a 12-step program and support. But, you're right, I'm probably going to need money to reach my goals. I mean, it's probably not going to be a big deal getting to meetings, as long as there's a bus around who can take me to the Congregational church on Center Street. But I do need to think about my long-term prospects. For now, though, I'd appreciate anything you can give me."

Ava took a deep breath. "Well, I need to get back to work. You're free to hang out here in this room or come down with me to talk to the guests. Whatever you want to do. And I'll take you to the store as soon as I'm done with work."

Jessica blinked her eyes rapidly. "Oh, I'm so sorry. I know you have a lot of work to do. I hope I'm not going to cause any trouble by being here."

"Don't worry. This is my house. Therefore, I can decide who stays at this house without asking anybody's permission. Of course, I always like to get input, but this is my decision."

Jessica closed her eyes as she lay on the bed. "Go on down. It's okay. I need a nap. As I said, I was down at the beach until 6 a.m., just walking. And then I took another six hours just to get the courage to knock on your door. So, I'm beat."

At that, Ava left.

What was she getting herself into?

CHAPTER 6

JESSICA

Jessica could not believe her good fortune. She loved this room so much, but it wasn't just that. She'd been living out of her van for the past year and half or so, so any room would be luxurious to her at this point. But this one really was. It had a fireplace, hardwood floors, a beautiful comfortable bed with soft sheets and blankets and pillowcases. There was a cherrywood chest of drawers for her to put her clothes, when she got some. There were candles and a little bubbling fountain.

And there was that picture. The picture that drew her in yet also repelled her somehow. It was a picture of some ladies and children in wooden shoes by a beach, and, while she didn't think she'd actually been on this beach, the picture spoke to her in some other way. But, try as she might, she couldn't understand what it was about this picture that was so important to her. Why was she so strongly drawn to it?

Ava had explained the meaning behind the picture, and apparently it was set in some long-ago time, judging by the way the people were dressed – the ladies were wearing scarves and peasant dresses and wooden shoes, and the children were wearing straw hats like they did over one hundred years ago. And Ava also explained that the picture was set on a beach in Brittany, France, a place Jessica had never been to. So, Jessica knew the picture didn't resonate because it was a beach she had visited.

No. There was something else about it. She couldn't put her finger on it, but she knew it was filled with hope and some other emotion buried deep within. Was it fear? Hate? Regret? She didn't know. And she didn't know why she didn't know.

She understood that the picture wasn't just one thing to her. It was many things, not all bad. So, while she was tempted to ask Ava to put the picture into a different part of the house, she didn't really want to. She wanted to just stare at it and feel.

Before she knew it, she was closing her eyes on the comfortable king-sized bed. She drifted off, and she had that dream. It was a dream she had just about every night. It was a woman, and she was pushing a very young girl on the swing. The girl was only about five years old, maybe a bit less, and she was dressed in a red coat-dress, white tights, and black Mary Janes on her chubby little feet.

The young girl swung, higher and higher, so high she felt she could touch the clouds. The young girl was laughing hysterically, and then she jumped off the swing into a pile of leaves. The woman scolded the young girl for getting her new coat dress dirty. But, the mother was also laughing, so she wasn't too angry with the little girl.

Jessica had the dream about that woman and child all the time. She didn't know who they were, so she had no idea why she would be dreaming about them so much. She only knew that this mother and child came to her whenever she closed her eyes.

Jessica's eyes opened, and she saw it was dark outside.

She'd arrived at this house early in the morning, so she must've been sleeping for a long time. And that was a good thing because she needed the sleep. She hadn't been sleeping well ever since she started living in that van. It was too uncomfortable in there and too noisy. And she never felt safe. Here, in this room, she finally felt safe, so she could finally rest her head.

She opened the door of her bedroom and padded downstairs. People were milling about in the foyer, and a guy was sitting in front of the fireplace. He had sandy blonde hair, a slim frame, and a kindly face. He wasn't all that tall – he was probably about her height, and she was 5'8". Soft blue eyes, his long blonde hair pulled up in a ponytail, a slight goatee.

People kept coming up to him and asking for his autograph, and everybody seemed very excited he was there. Jessica surmised that maybe this guy was somehow famous. If he was, she didn't recognize him.

Yet, he seemed so familiar...

She approached him because she wanted to get a better look at him. Right as she did, he looked at her and smiled. "Hello," he said in a friendly manner. "My name's Andrew."

"Jessica," she said politely. "Uh, I don't want to be rude, but I was wondering. People were asking for your autograph. Are you somebody?"

He laughed. "My name is Andrew Jameson, if that tells you anything."

Jessica narrowed her eyes. She understood that there was an up-and-coming musician named Andrew Jameson. A guy who was being talked about like he was the next Ed Sheeran. She remembered seeing something about him in *Rolling Stone* magazine, no less. That was a magazine she read all the time, because she really got into the long articles it published.

And, come to think of it, he does look familiar.

THE BEACHSIDE REUNION..

But there was something else about this guy that was familiar. She just couldn't put her finger on it. "Andrew Jameson. You don't happen to be the same-"

He nodded his head. "Yes. One and the same."

"Oh," Jessica said. "What brings you here?"

"I'm hiding out from my record producer. Not to mention my agent. They've been on my rear about getting some more music out, and I keep telling them that the more they're on my rear, the less likely they will get anything good out of me. I don't work well under pressure like that."

She knew about pressure. When she was in college, she was always putting a lot of pressure on herself to make the best grades. But that time seemed so long ago at this point.

He smiled. His teeth were perfectly straight, and Jessica noticed his lips were full and bee-stung, like Brad Pitt's. She also noticed his eyes weren't necessarily completely blue. Rather, they were flecked with hazel and green, and she saw in those eyes that this guy was full of mirth and fun. At any rate, when he smiled, she felt a light that shot through her and went all the way down to her toes. It had been so long since she'd been around somebody who just exuded positive energy. The only kind of energy that she ever got from her stepmother and father was negative. The only thing they could ever do was tell her how disappointed they were in her.

She always wished she'd really known her mother. But her mother had died when Jessica was only four years old. She was killed in some accident that her father would never talk about. Jessica asked him many times about her mother, and what happened to her, but her father would always change the subject.

She didn't really have any memories of her mother. In fact, she didn't have any memories of her childhood except for one birthday at a park. Something happened on that birthday that was in her locked box, somewhere in the deep recesses of her mind. She didn't know. She tried to go back to this park many times. She asked her father about her fifth birthday and where it took place. He was always so uncomfortable when she would ask that question. And, once again, he'd change the subject.

She found out where the park was when she found one of her scrapbooks. It was a baby book, and her mother had written about her plans for Jessica's fifth birthday. Included in the baby book was the invitation that would be sent out to all her little friends. So, she went to that park many times because she just had to get answers. And, when she would go to that place, she would feel an overwhelming sense of dread. The dread was just leaping at her from all directions - from the trees, the pond, the grass. The quacking ducks seemed to be mocking her.

She could sense it. But she just couldn't put her finger on it. Much like she just couldn't put her finger on why this guy seemed so familiar.

She realized she was just staring at this guy. He'd said something to her, and she didn't pay attention to what he said. "I'm so sorry, I went outer limits just now. What did you just say?"

"Nothing. I just said I was drawn to this house because it's so close to the beach. I can hear the waves rolling in from my window. It's also very appealing that it has balconies and fireplaces in all the rooms. And, like I said, I just needed a place close to the beach where I can be alone and write some music and words."

Jessica scratched her shoulder nervously. It had been over a week since she had a fix of her OxyContin. She gave it up cold turkey, which was probably the hardest thing she'd ever done. But she knew she had to do that before coming to ask Ava to stay. She got through the worst of the physical withdrawal - the puking, the chills, the sleepless nights, the racing heart, the muscle cramps that would hit out of nowhere and would immobilize her. That was really the easy part.

The hard part was getting through the mental pain of kicking the drug. She'd started to convince herself she actually needed to be on this drug, because she felt so badly about herself when she wasn't. There was some kind of deep psychic wound that penetrated her everyday life when she wasn't high. It had always been there for as long as she could remember.

Jessica nodded. "Yeah, I know what you mean. I don't write songs or anything like that, but being by a beach is very calming for me as well."

He smiled. "Jessica, it's great to meet you. And I feel I know you somehow. I can't put my finger on it. Did you grow up around here?"

"I did, as a matter of fact. At least I spent my early years here. I don't really remember them. I grew up in the Los Angeles area, at least after I was about five years old or so."

He started to laugh. "Oh, my. You and I have the same story. I grew up here too, at least until I was five years old. And then I moved to Florida with my mother. How crazy. Both of us spent our early childhood here, and then both of us moved away to a big city. And now, here we both are. It's crazy how life works sometimes, isn't it?"

Jessica just nodded her head, feeling that crazy connection to him. It was almost as if they were bound together by something, but she didn't know what. "Yeah, imagine that. It's like we're reunited after..."

Jessica had no idea how to complete that thought. And she had no idea why she used the term reunited. Just because the two of them had grown up on the same island, and had moved away at the same time in their lives, didn't mean they actually knew each other when they were young.

Did it?

Andrew cocked his head. "Jessica, I know this will sound forward because I just met you, but would you like to go to the beach with me?"

"Yes," Jessica said. "I would."

The two walked to the beach and sat down on the sand. Jessica breathed in the salty air and tried to relax. She felt like she was out of practice with social graces. After all, she had lived the last few years on the streets. She certainly wasn't prepared to make conversation with a stranger.

Andrew breathed deeply and let it out. And then he closed his eyes, and laid back. "This could work. This could definitely work. I can't tell you the last time I've felt this relaxed. That's definitely what I need in my life at the moment. Relaxation. Low stress. Some people can produce their best work when they're high-strung and on edge, but that's not me. My music is mellow and sunny. So I definitely have to have the right vibes to produce."

Jessica nodded her head. She had a feeling that her initial impression about this guy was correct. Just like he said his music wasn't dark, but was more sunny, his demeanor seemed to be the same. She started to relax just a little bit as she sat next to him.

"So, you're more Jack Johnson than Eddie Vedder, then."

Andrew nodded his head. "You might say that. Maybe I'll play you some music? I mean, after I get settled in my room and everything. If it's not going to bother anybody, I kinda plan to come out here this evening and work on some stuff. It always helps me to have an audience."

Jessica could think of nothing she would've liked more for that evening. For just a brief moment, while she was sitting here with this guy, she didn't feel the siren song of OxyContin beckoning her. She just felt like she could lose herself in the moment. Yet, she was just a little shy about taking this guy up on his offer. So she didn't actually address it.

"What's your inspiration for your music?" she asked him.

He shrugged his shoulders. "For the longest time, it was therapy. I had issues in my past. From the time of my early childhood. So, I didn't really fit in that much in my school or with my neighborhood. My uncle bought me a guitar and taught me about music, and, I don't know, I really took to it."

Jessica could relate to early childhood trauma. Although, she didn't really know exactly why she could relate to it. That was still a mystery to her. But maybe that was the reason why she was feeling such a magnetic pull toward this guy. He had early childhood trauma, and she did too. A part of her knew that.

"So, the music was therapy for you. But you just told me your music was sunny, upbeat. I guess I don't really understand that. I always thought that traumatic upbringings resulted in dark lyrics."

She thought about Kurt Cobain, a singer that had always fascinated her. He had a traumatic childhood because of his parent's divorce and his stepfather abusing his mother in front of him, resulting in the dark and angry lyrics that were a hallmark of that particular group.

Andrew smiled. "Well, my music was a way of catharsis. But now, I want it to be sunny and positive. I have to start looking at the bright things in life. Otherwise I would end up in a very dark hole. And I don't want to end up in that kind of hole, so I need to pretend, now, that my outside environment is unicorns and rainbows. So, you're right, I could channel my inner depression towards my music, and I have. But now I'm choosing to go the other way."

Jessica clasped her hands in front of her. She desperately wished she had some kind of artistic outlet for her own trauma like Andrew did. She could never sing a note, didn't really know how to read music, and artistically? She could draw stick figures, and even those were not all that good.

The only time she felt peaceful was when she was out on the water. When she used to surf and scuba dive. Those were the best times of her life. That was why she applied to the graduate program at Boston University, which had the best marine biology program in the country. She was accepted for their graduate program based on her undergraduate grades and because she got her BS in marine biology at that same school. She was a very good student. She got straight A's, and she did extremely well on her entrance exam.

That was all before her accident, of course. After the accident, she couldn't even function.

"Do you surf?" she asked him.

He smiled. "Of course. I grew up in Florida, always in the water. I learned to surf when I was 5 years old. And there's just something about being on the water that inspires me. I don't know, it makes me feel like I'm part of a larger whole. I guess I can never stop being awed by the size of the ocean and thinking that, somewhere on the horizon, there's some faraway land like Africa. I don't know. It makes me feel more connected to the earth in some way."

Jessica was amazed that Andrew seemed to be articulating her own thoughts. It was like she was looking into a mirror, except this mirror reflected back a much sunnier person. It was like he was the person she wished she could be. He had childhood trauma. Yet he was seemingly much more functional than she was. Why couldn't she get her act together?"

She nodded her head. "I know what you mean. In my case, I really love to be on the water, but also in the water. It seems like the world underwater is so different from the world on land."

She still remembered her first scuba diving trip, back

when she was only 10 years old. She was terrified at first. She had some experience in the water, with scuba equipment, from an early age. But this was her first time actually diving with the gear, and she was nervous. However, she was so amazed at what she saw that she didn't want to come up. The schools of fish, the underwater coral, the sea horses and sea turtles and the bright colors that she didn't think she would ever see under the water. A friendly and curious sea lion came within inches of her face, so close she thought she could touch him. And for years, she thought about the sea lion and how much she wanted him to be her pet.

After that first experience, she was hooked. She always wanted to pretend that the underwater domain was the world. Somehow, her life was more of a fantasy underwater. It was like she was a mermaid. She'd always gotten lost as a young girl in tales of heroic sailors and beautiful mermaids. She couldn't get enough of those tales from all over the world. She vaguely remembered her mother reading her stories about the beautiful creatures. Somehow, the mermaids just seemed so free. As if nothing in this world could touch them, and if they were threatened, they could just swim away from the danger. She desperately wished that nothing in this world could touch her, as well.

Somehow, it just seemed the world underwater was just different from this world. There wasn't the same violence. The same ugliness. The same kind of hatred that she saw in too many people. There was nothing down there except for beautiful, friendly and innocuous creatures. Well, she knew that many of the creatures were not so innocuous, like the man-eating sharks and barracudas, but she never encountered them. It was as if she had gone to Jurassic Park, but only encountered the Brontosauruses and not the T-Rexes.

"Well, maybe you and I can go surfing in the mornings," Andrew said. "I like to start the day by taking to the water right after dawn. Even when the waves aren't that great, it's just kind of liberating to be out there. You mentioned you're going to be staying here, too? You said that, right?"

Jessica nodded her head. She didn't really know how to explain exactly why she would be staying there, however. How could she possibly tell him that she would be staying here because the owner of the house felt sorry for her because she was homeless? She really liked this guy. She could see herself bonding with him as a friend. She knew he was a kindred spirit. She didn't want to admit she was a homeless person with a drug problem until this very morning.

"Yes. I'm going to be kind of a utility worker, so to speak. The owner needed somebody who could do anything needed to pitch in, so that's me. I guess I'm gonna be kind of a maid, cook, laundress type person."

He nodded his head. "Good for you. If it means you get to stay in a beautiful place like this, it's worth it to do anything that they want you to do."

As Jessica looked at Andrew, she tried to remember what she had read about him. The article she'd read was in *Rolling Stone*, and he only had one CD out. Yet, it seemed then he was a rising superstar, at least the way the magazine described him. There was a hope that he would usher in his brand of mellow pop rock as a new standard for the coming music era. Like the 60s were dominated by Motown and rock' n' roll, the 70s were dominated by disco, arena rock and soft rock, the 80s were marked by synth pop and New Wave, the 90s was the era of the grunge, the 2000s belonged to the straight pop artists, and the 2010s seemed to be the domain of R&B and rap.

Somehow, the pendulum was swinging back around, and artists who had the sound of the 1970s era Dan Fogelberg or Christopher Cross were slaying the charts once more.

Although Jessica never actually heard Andrew's music, she read that he was in the lane of Dan Fogelberg or James Taylor. Which suited Jessica just fine because she was so anxious to hear something other than rap and R&B, and get back to the music of singer-songwriters who had a softer edge.

"I agree. I mean, I'm really looking forward to working here and staying here." Then she let out a breath.

A couple of girls came over to James and gleefully asked for his autograph on their volleyball. James had a pen on him, which he probably always did because the autograph thing was undoubtedly a daily occurrence, and he signed it.

"I probably should be getting back up to the house. I feel a song coming on, and I have to get on it when the muse moves me. But it's really great meeting you. I hope you take me up on my offer to come down to the beach with me in the evenings and listen to my new music."

"I'd love to," Jessica said. "I'm honored that you would-"

"Use you as a guinea pig?" he said with a smile.

"Well, I don't necessarily think of myself as a guinea pig, but I'm just so happy that I get to hear your new stuff." She hated to admit she wasn't familiar with his current stuff, let alone his new stuff, so she didn't say anything. She sometimes listened to the radio in her van, but she tended to listen to the oldies stations because somehow they reminded her of her mother. Again, she couldn't quite put a finger on why this music reminded her of her mother. It was just a feeling she had whenever she listened to songs from the 70s or 80s - she could almost smell her mother's perfume when she listened to this music. And that made her feel safe.

She quietly went to her own room and lay down on the bed. She once more stared at the painting on the wall. It was somehow associated with something extremely painful, but at the same time, it was associated with healing. Or, rather, an attempt to heal herself. So, in this way, the painting was soothing to her more than anything else.

She closed her eyes, trying to figure out why she had so many senses of déjà vu. Why Andrew seemed so familiar to her, why did this painting mean so much to her, what was it about that park that was so scary for her?

Somehow, she knew in her heart that Andrew held the key to all of this. But she was just going to have to get these answers later.

CHAPTER 7

Ava couldn't believe her luck. Andrew Jameson, The Andrew Jameson, the singer she was gaga about, was staying there. She really felt like the Queen of England or something. Like, out of all the places in town that he could go to, he chose her place. She never dreamed she could get such a luminous star in her midst, let alone stay with her.

She was going to have to call Quinn and Hallie. She'd call Sarah, but Sarah was, once more, on the West Coast, finalizing some winery contracts.

Quinn, Hallie and Ava were huge fans of Andrew Jameson. Even though Andrew only had two CDs out, he was right up their alley. Ava had to admit that probably one of the reasons she was so excited about Andrew's music was that he sounded so much like the early 70s soft rock she grew up with as a child. Growing up, her favorite musical acts were Air Supply, Barry Manilow, The Carpenters, Christopher Cross and Dan Fogelberg. It wasn't that she wasn't into the harder acts from the 70s, like Journey, Van Halen, REO, Styx and Kansas – in fact, she recently saw REO Speedwagon in concert at the county fair, and she knew every word to every song. But the songs of her youth were mellow, by and large, songs she could really sing along with.

Andrew Jameson was a throwback to those times. Somehow when she listened to his music, she felt like she was nine years old, sitting on her bed and listening to her K-Tel records, or at the roller rink, which was where all the kids her age went to on the weekends, or in her aunt's Olds that constantly smelled like cigarette smoke. It was summers at the beach in South Carolina, traveling out there in the back part of her uncle's enormous gold Gran Torino - not in the backseat, but in the "very very back," as she and her sister put it, for those were the days before seat belt laws restricted kids from traveling in this part of the car. It was days spent traveling in the ancient Valiant car, with the duct tape covering the rips in the vinyl backseat and the paint that came off on her fingers when she rubbed the side of the car.

Weekends at her aunt's farm, going with them to eat cheese and sausage grinders at Mario's restaurant in Westport, going with them to Silver Dollar City in the Ozarks, going to drive-in movies with them – those were the memories that were invoked whenever Ava thought about that time in her life. Those were the memories Andrew Jameson's music brought to her. And now she would be able to entertain him right under her very own roof.

When she called Quinn and told her the news, she squealed with delight. "Oh my Goddess, I don't believe it. I mean, I do believe it, because you're telling me, but that has to be the craziest thing I've ever heard. How did you score that?"

"I don't know. All I can say is he's in his room right this very second, if he's not already down at the beach."

Ava immediately invited Quinn to come over, and told her to bring Hallie, too. Quinn told Ava that the two were going to be right over. "I'm so excited!" Quinn enthused.

* * *

Later on that evening, after Quinn and Hallie had come over and met Andrew, and he couldn't have been more gracious to her two friends, they all made a plan to meet out on the beach and do a sing-along, including Jessica.

Andrew was trying to be low-key about the entire thing, because he didn't want anybody to know who he was, so he wore a hat over his eyes and sunglasses, even though it was 8 o'clock in the evening, so it was quite dark outside. They all built a bonfire and Andrew sang his songs while Ava, Quinn and Hallie sang along, as all three of the women knew all of his songs by heart. Jessica, for her part, didn't know any of his songs, but she seemed to sway along to music and really enjoy herself.

Ava smiled as she saw Andrew and Jessica stealing glances at one another. Andrew would look at Jessica while he sang and Jessica would look at him, just a glance, and then she would quickly look away. And then Jessica would look at Andrew, and the look in her eyes was unmistakable. Ava knew that look anywhere. It was a look she used to see in Daniel's eyes. Daniel was a really good guy. In fact, if he wasn't killed in a car accident, Ava knew they would still be married to this day. She knew what she had with Daniel was a love at first sight kind of thing, a lightning bolt that struck her from the moment she looked into his green eyes, and she knew from the look on his face he felt the same way about her. Looking at Jessica, Ava saw that same look in her eyes - she was definitely struck by lightning. And, by the looks of Andrew, he felt the same way.

The five of them stayed on the beach until 2 o'clock in the morning, singing songs and toasting marshmallows that Ava didn't eat. Ava thought that evening was probably one of the best of her entire life.

He couldn't wait to tell Deacon about Andrew staying

there. She doubted Deacon knew who Andrew was, but she didn't care. She was just going to have to play his music for Deacon the next time she saw her handsome boyfriend. And that's what he was, really, to her - her boyfriend. And she couldn't be more thrilled about that.

No doubt about it, her life was looking up. For the first time in her life, things were good with her mother. Things were fantastic with Deacon. Her bed-and-breakfast was thriving so much that an internationally known pop star wanted to stay with her.

How could she possibly ask for anything more?

CHAPTER 8

SAMANTHA

Samantha got the job at the Blue Moon Surfside bakery and deli, as she knew she would. She liked working at the deli because the sandwiches were divine and she got a discount on them. But that Friday was an event she really was looking forward to - her first catering party.

She was outfitted with a cute catering uniform consisting of a black skirt, a white tuxedo shirt and a bow tie. The event she was working was a silent auction benefit dinner. The cause was ALS Research, and the hostess of the party was a woman named Ellen Ripley.

Ellen was known to be one of the doyennes of the island. Her billionaire husband Noah was a founder of a green tech giant that provided alternative energy to countries worldwide. Before he founded his company, called Greengenix, he was a hedge fund manager. The couple lived in New York City and had a summer home on the North Shore of Nantucket.

Most exciting for Samantha was that the Ripleys had two sons and three daughters. One of the sons, Adrian, was 27 and was a trust-fund baby worth millions. Adrian was, at the moment, single, having broken up with a supermodel-type woman named Naomi Harris.

Before Samantha worked the event, she spent time online looking up all she could find about the handsome Adrian. She hoped he would be at the event. She found out he was the proud owner of a 60-foot yacht called Big Nauti and apparently had homes in Boston, Switzerland and Nantucket.

As far as what he did for a living, Samantha discerned he didn't do much. He didn't have to work, and he apparently decided not to. But that didn't matter to Samantha. In fact, it was a plus for her. If he didn't have a job, he would have all the time in the world for her.

She imagined a life, just the two of them, sailing around the world. They would lay around a pool in Monte Carlo during the day and play the tables at night. They'd boogie-board down sand dunes in New Zealand (yes, that's a thing), see The Temple of the Sun in Machu Picchu, and visit castles in Prague.

A life of travel and adventure and never worrying about running out of money sounded like heaven on earth to Samantha. So, she knew she would set her sights on Adrian when she worked the ALS fundraiser.

So, that Friday at 4, she was getting ready for her party. She made sure her blue eyes stood out with smoky-grey eye shadow, false eyelashes that she purchased from Target before she got to Nantucket, and black eyeliner. She evened out her complexion with the perfect shade of ivory foundation that matched her natural skin tone to a T. Rose-colored lipstick completed the look.

She liked how she looked with her hair up, so she swept it up in a tight chignon. Then she went to Grayson's full-view mirror - Grayson had moved all of his furniture into his new room in the granny flat, and he, fortunately, had a nice mirror hanging in his closet - and admired the way she looked.

Grayson was lying on his bed, reading a book, when Samantha barged on in.

"Hey," he said. "You look cute. And, no, that skirt doesn't make your butt look big. I know that's what you're about to ask me."

"Am I that predictable?" Samantha asked, thinking that the skirt actually did make her butt look a little wide. She was self-conscious about her figure, even though she knew she shouldn't be. When she looked in the mirror, she saw shoulders that were too broad, hips that were too flared, and breasts too small.

She was 5'4 and 115 pounds, so she knew she shouldn't be so hard on herself. But she was. What she wouldn't give to be tall and slim like Gigi Hadid or to have an interesting face like Carla Delevingne with the hella cool eyebrows.

Her face absolutely bored her to tears. There was nothing unique about it. There wasn't a strong nose or huge eyes or enormous Angelina Jolie pillow lips. She just looked so average.

She shook her head. She would have to tell herself she was beautiful and unique and hope she'd get some confidence and eventually believe it.

Fake it until you make it, she thought.

She turned around and smiled. "So, Grayson, wish me luck. This is my first big society gig! There will be a silent auction, an open bar, and a live four-piece jazz band. My boss Javier told me that anybody who was anybody on this island will be at this function tonight." She clapped her hands together. "Maybe tonight, I'll meet my prince."

"I hope you do," Grayson said.

"And what are you going to be doing tonight?" Samantha asked him.

Grayson shrugged. "I'll be working on my novel," he said. "What I always do anymore, it seems like."

Samantha went and sat down on the end of his bed. "Gray, you need to get out there yourself. Make some friends, go to the bars, meet the woman who will make your heart go pitter-patter." She patted his knee. "Or you could always get a Bumble date."

He rolled his eyes. "Like you've had such great luck on Bumble," he said. "No, thanks. I'm cool, Sam, staying in and writing. But you have fun."

"I will," Samantha said, taking one last look at herself in the mirror. "Okay, I'm off."

CHAPTER 9

SAMANTHA

Samantha arrived at the beautiful Cape Cod mansion that apparently was valued at over $50 million and took her orders. She set up the tables and got the buffet table ready to go. Then she went to the kitchen, where chefs were preparing appetizers to serve to the guests.

The place was gorgeous inside, full of huge flower arrangements and ice sculptures shaped like swans and flying horses. She was one of a hundred cater waiters doing the same things she was doing - setting up chairs and rolling silverware and helping get the appetizers ready to go.

At 6 PM, the guests started to pour in, and Samantha was busy running to get more appetizers for her platter and taking drink orders. Everybody was dressed to the nines in this place, for it was a white-tie event. The men were dressed in white-tie tuxedos, and the women were all decked out in floor-length gowns. Most of the women wore a ton of makeup and had long hair swooped up on their heads in tight chignons.

But there were a few women who let their long hair flow, mainly the younger ones. Samantha was impressed by how fit and trim almost every woman was in the room. The men were, too, but a few had paunches and skinny legs. It was obvious to her, however, it was almost a requirement that wealthy women stay in shape.

Adrian arrived a little after 7, apparently fashionably late. Samantha took a breath and approached him with her tray full of flutes full of Prosecco.

"Hello," she said to him, making eye contact. "Would you like a glass of Prosecco?"

He smiled and took one of her glasses, nodded his head and kept talking to the group he was with.

Samantha was discouraged. She had it in her head that when he saw her, he would hear the love theme from Romeo and Juliet playing in the background as he saw she was the woman of his dreams.

Yes, she was a servant and he was wealthy. But she'd read enough romance novels to know that that kind of power imbalance was like catnip to wealthy men. She rarely read stories about wealthy men falling for wealthy women. It was usually a poor college girl or bartender catching the eye of an international billionaire, like Ana and Grey and countless knock-off stories that followed that particular trilogy.

So, why wouldn't she be able to attract the attention of Adrian? She was just going to have to try harder.

At 8, the silent auction was closed, and a speaker took the stage while everyone took their seats. After that, the guests lined up at the buffet and piled their plates with Lobster Thermidor, Beef Bourguignon, Lobster Newberg, Chicken Fricassée and Linguine with Clam Sauce. Samantha looked longingly at the food as she ran to get more of it, replacing the chafers when they went empty and keeping her eye on Adrian, hoping for any sign he noticed her.

Samantha was disappointed to see that every time she looked at Adrian, he was talking to somebody else and not looking her way at all. She felt tears coming to her eyes as she berated herself for being so stupid. Who was she kidding? She was 24 and had dated only losers. She told herself she just never had the time to meet somebody special, and that was partly true.

But maybe she just didn't have *it*. She didn't have what it took to catch the eye of the type of guy who she wanted to attract. Maybe the romance novels were really just silly escapism, a way to sell books by giving girls like her hope that wealthy men truly were looking for poor women. Maybe the books were just retelling the Cinderella myth, over and over and over again, and weren't really based on reality at all.

*****

After the event was over, Samantha went to the beach. The Ripley home was right on the Miacomet Beach, so it was on the South Shore, where the waves were active, and the surf was high. It was midnight, and scattered groups were sitting around fire rings, and there were quite a few guests from the ALS fundraiser walking along the shore in their finery.

It was dark outside, and since there was a new moon, there wasn't even moonlight to brighten up the beach. Samantha got a little too close to the water and an enormous wave came in and swept her off her feet. The undertow was powerful and, before she knew what was happening, she found herself in deep, savage water, far away from the shore.

She frantically tried to swim her way back, but she was caught in a riptide, and, no matter how hard she tried to swim, she found herself getting further and further out. And, since she was fully clothed, including her shoes, she felt herself getting weighed down. It would've been impossible for her to swim out of the riptide even if she was in a bathing suit. But being fully clothed, she knew it was a hopeless situation.

She put her arms up and cried out, hoping that somebody from the shore would come out and save her. Then she felt herself going under.

The next thing she knew, she was lying on the beach, and a man was pounding on her chest and giving her mouth to mouth. She took an enormous breath, spitting out the water accumulated in her lungs. There was a group of people around her, all of them dressed in fine gowns and tuxedos, all of them staring at her with a mixture of horror and, when she opened her eyes, relief. One tall blonde woman put her hand to her chest and took a deep breath as she stared at the now-conscious Samantha.

The man helping her came into focus, and Samantha saw it was Adrian. He was shirtless and in his underwear with no shoes. He smiled when Samantha opened her eyes and coughed up a lungful of water.

"Thank God," he said. His face was close to hers and she could smell his cologne. It was a delicious scent, full of spice and wood, with just a hint of lemon and bergamot. His dark wavy hair was wet and in his face. His beautiful brown eyes with the long, long eyelashes, were staring at her.

She stood up, looking at Adrian, her white knight, in awe.

"What happened?" she asked him, vaguely remembering she almost drowned. But she couldn't, for the life of her, remember how she got into the water in the first place.

"You were standing by the water and a huge wave came in and knocked you for a loop," Adrian said. "And the next thing I knew, you were way out to sea and shouting and raising your arms. So, I swam out to you and got you out of the water."

"You saved me," Samantha said. "Thank you."

"Not a problem," he said. "I'm just glad you're okay."

Samantha nodded her head.

"Yes, thank you," Samantha said. Then she took a deep breath. "Um, I think I need to get home and lay down." She felt exhausted. After all, it wasn't every day that you almost die.

Adrian nodded his head. "No offense, but I don't know if you're in any shape to drive," he said. "I can take you home."

Samantha's blue eyes got wide. Was this really happening? Was she finally taking a starring role in a romance novel? Was her dream finally coming true?

"Oh, I can drive," Samantha said, knowing that, in every romance novel she'd ever read, the girl played hard to get at first. She usually made the wealthy guy pursue her, which always made her more desirable. "But thank you."

Adrian shook his head. "No, you just had a huge shock. I agree, you should probably get home as soon as possible. It's getting pretty cold out, and you probably need a hot shower and a warm blanket."

Samantha nodded her head, not wanting to press the issue further. "Well, thank you," she said. "I live inland in Naushop, so it's not very far at all."

And this was true, as Naushop was a neighboring enclave to Miacomet, which was where the Ripley mansion was.

"Yes, you aren't far," Adrian said. "By the way, my name is Adrian Ripley."

"Samantha Flynn," Sam said, her heart soaring.

Adrian went over to his clothes, and Samantha noticed how ripped his body was. She found herself admiring his toned chest and abs and the way his leg muscles were sinewy and glistening in the light of a neighboring fire ring.

He got dressed and put his suit coat around her shoulders. She wrapped the coat around her tighter as she followed him back to the Ripley house, where his white Range Rover was parked.

A white Range Rover. My prince doesn't ride a white horse, he drives a white Range Rover. It was almost coming together too perfectly.

He opened the door, and Samantha sat down on the buttery leather seat. She directed him to her home, and they arrived. He helped her out of the car and went and knocked on the door of the granny flat. Samantha had forgotten her house key when she left that day, which was just like her. She should've put the key on the key chain, but she didn't get around to it.

Grayson opened the door, took one look at Samantha and his face became immediately concerned. "Sam, what happened? You're all wet."

Samantha looked over at Adrian, hoping he could explain what happened.

"Samantha here had a little accident," Adrian said. "She got a little too close to the water, and an enormous wave swept her out."

Samantha nodded her head. "And Adrian saved me," she said. "I would've died if Adrian didn't strip off all his clothes and dive into that cold water to stop me from drowning."

Samantha was aware she probably sounded way too excited when she recounted how she almost died, but she was beside herself with joy that Adrian was the one who saved her, and he was enough of a gentleman to bring her home.

Grayson nodded his head. "I see."

"Okay, my work is done," Adrian said. "I think Samantha's in good hands, so I'll be shuffling off."

"Thank you so much," Samantha said, once again feeling disappointed. She imagined that maybe he would've asked her out. But that didn't seem to be what was going to happen.

"Not a problem," he said. "Bye now."

Then he left.

Samantha saw Grayson was ready with a warm blanket and he was building a fire in the fireplace.

"I'm sorry, Gray," Samantha said. "But you'll have to drive me to my car tomorrow."

"Of course, I'll do that. You've had a horrible night," Grayson said. "So, you can sleep in my bed and I'll take the air mattress tonight."

"No, that's okay," Samantha said. "I mean, I don't mind the air mattress."

"I insist," Grayson said. "Now, get in the shower, and I'll bring you your warm pajamas. You look like you're about to freeze to death."

Samantha didn't even realize how cold she was because she was so busy focusing on her white knight that she didn't think about anything else.

But, now that Adrian was gone, she felt the cold. And, for the first time, she felt the belated panic about how she had almost died in that dark, cold water.

"Grayson, I almost died," she said. "I mean, if Adrian didn't come out there and bring me out, I would've drowned."

She felt her heart pounding as she thought about her panic in the water. She was a strong swimmer, but not when there was a riptide and not when she was fully clothed. She'd almost died once before in her life - she was 3 years old and got the membrane of an orange caught in her throat. She couldn't breathe and if she didn't have a small enough hand that she could pull the orange membrane out, she would've choked to death.

Now, here was her second near-death experience, and she was feeling it.

Grayson tried to make a joke. "Sam, since you've come through 24 years acting like there's no such thing as danger,

I'm surprised that near-death experiences aren't a daily occurrence."

"Ha ha, Gray," Samantha said. "My near-drowning isn't a laughing matter. Or maybe to you it is." Then she rolled her eyes. "I'm going to turn in. I'll take you up on sleeping in your bed."

"Samantha, I'm sorry. I was being insensitive. Now, tell me how you're feeling right now."

That was Grayson. He really cared about how she was feeling.

"Well, Grayson, it was scary as hell," she said. "All I remember was that I was thinking about my mom, and about how sad she would be about my death. You don't know how it feels to be stranded in the middle of the ocean, trapped in a riptide and going under. You think, 'this is it. This is how it ends.'"

Grayson silently laid her pajamas on the coffee table and presented her with a huge towel. "I know how you feel," he said. "When I was in high school, I worked at a convenience store, and I had a gun pointed at me. I felt the same way. I thought about my mother and how I hadn't really had a chance to live. How unfair that was."

Samantha nodded her head. "I mean, it doesn't seem that I was conscious in the water all that long, not even a couple of minutes. But it seemed like everything went in slow motion. Was it like that for you, too? Did it seem like time stood still?"

Grayson smiled. "Yes! I've always heard that, you know. Like right before a big car accident or something like that, everything seems to slow down. The car that's coming at you going 70 miles per hour seems like it's going like 5 miles per hour. I guess it's the same way when you have a near-death experience."

"Right," Samantha said. "By the way, your story is awful, Grayson. What happened?"

"The cops came," he said. "And the next day, when I had pancakes, they tasted like the best pancakes in the entire world. Everything in my world seemed brighter and more colorful. I kissed my little brother when I got home and my parents, and told all of them how much I loved them. I had this amazing outlook for like a week or so, but, as time passed, that incredible outlook became less and less. So, when you're faced with death and you cheat it, you don't have this amazing appreciation of life for too long."

Samantha took a deep breath. "I don't have that outlook just yet, but I probably will. At any rate, I think I need a hot bath and my warm pajamas and my air mattress."

"Sam, I told you that you can sleep in my bed," Grayson protested.

"I know you did, and I'm telling you no. The air mattress is fine. But if you want to do something nice, you can draw me a bubble bath."

Grayson smiled and went into the bathroom. In a matter of minutes, the tub was full of suds, and Samantha shooed Grayson off so that she could get in.

Samantha sunk into the warm water and truly let herself think about her close call.

And that thought made her sob like she hadn't for a long, long time.

CHAPTER 10

SAMANTHA

The night that Samantha was at the high-society function, Grayson was alone, doing what he usually did when Samantha wasn't around. He wrote about her. He was working on a sci-fi fantasy novel, and the main character in this novel was based on Samantha.

The heroine in his novel, whose name was Alina, had the same quirks as Samantha. She liked the same kinds of foods, the same type of music, and had the same sense of humor. And, of course, the hero and romantic interest that he drew up in his novel was based on him. He knew he was safe and that Samantha would never know how he felt about her, even if she read his book. He knew Samantha would probably never recognize herself on the printed page. But he got her.

He knew everything about her. He knew she cried when there was a happy ending in a movie, even more than a sad one. He knew how embarrassed she was that her second toe was slightly longer than the first one. That was the reason why she'd never wear open-toed sandals. He knew her guilty pleasures were 70s soft rock artists such as Barry Manilow and The Carpenters and that she could sing along, albeit off-key, to every one of their songs. He knew she secretly longed to have been a cheerleader in her high school, but she just wasn't good enough to make it.

He also knew she was an artist in her heart, and she really wanted to become a cake decorator but didn't feel she had what it took to make it in that field. Still, it seemed she really wanted to aspire to that, for she religiously watched all the cake decorating shows on Netflix, including the brand-new one hosted by Mikey Day called *Is It Cake?*

Sugar Rush, The Great British Bake-Off, Bake Squad, Best Baker in America - she watched them all both on the Food Network and Netflix. Grayson didn't want her to spend her life watching the shows because he knew how discouraged she felt when watching them. Still, he didn't try to dissuade her from binging on these shows because they made her happy.

He'd seen some of the sketches that she'd drawn of the cakes that she'd like to make, and he knew she had a talent for decoration. She seemed to know just what colors go well with each other and what flowers to use. He'd seen her sketches for wedding cakes with roses, lilies, sprigs of greenery, seashells, butterflies and baby's breath for the more traditional weddings. And he also saw how she sketched different creative cakes that would go with couples who wanted something a little bit left of center or *avant-garde*. One of his favorite of her sketches was a three-tiered cake with Monet's water lilies painted on the sides. Another one of the cakes she drew had hearts, skulls and crossbones. It was a design that would make the late designer Christian Audigier, the inventor of the Ed Hardy label, cry with joy.

It was a miracle she even wanted to become best friends with him. He had a crush on her from the first time he saw her. She'd been looking for a roommate on Craig's List and he answered her ad and was stunned by her beauty.

However, he saw that she, with all her young-Goldie-Hawn gorgeousness and vivaciousness, would never go for an awkward guy like him. Not that he was bad-looking. His dark wavy hair sometimes got just a little too long, and he wore glasses, as he couldn't wear contacts because of astigmatism. Plus, he was just a little on the skinny side. His nose was slightly long, and his eyes were just a tiny bit too close together. But, all in all, he looked in the mirror, and he didn't hate what he saw. And, after he met her, he started hitting the gym, thinking that that might turn her head. Now he was still slim but muscular.

Not that she ever noticed or cared.

He was in love with her but knew she didn't feel the same way. But he always wanted the best for her because he wanted her to be happy.

So, when Samantha was brought home by Adrian from the beach and, even though she had a near-death experience, it was obvious she was smitten with the guy, Grayson's heart broke just a little. Grayson would give anything to have Samantha look at him the way she looked at the wealthy Adrian.

Then, when she got out of her bath, her skin pruning a little because she'd been in the tub for so long, she knocked softly on the door of his bedroom and then walked in before he said anything. That was Samantha for you - she'll knock to be polite, but she won't wait for the answer before barging in. And even that rather annoying trait charmed him because it was Samantha wielding the bad behavior.

To him, Sam could do no wrong.

"Grayson," Samantha said. "I know it's really late, but I have to talk to you."

Grayson sat up in his bed, looking expectantly at Samantha. He didn't say anything, and Sam came and sat on the end of his bed.

"Do you think it would be too forward for me to invite Adrian out for dinner? I found him on Facebook just now, and I could send him a message."

Grayson sighed. He was afraid of something like this.

"No, not too forward," he said. "After all, the guy saved your life."

Samantha's face brightened up. "That's what I was thinking! I mean, it's the perfect excuse, isn't it?"

"Yes, the perfect excuse," Grayson said without enthusiasm. "Where are you going to take him to dinner? Assuming he takes you up on your offer."

"I was thinking The Straight Wharf," Samantha said.

Grayson raised his eyebrows. "The Straight Wharf? Samantha, do you have the money for that place?"

Samantha shrugged. "No. But I was just approved for a credit card. It has a 29% interest rate, an annual fee of $100 and it has a $250 credit limit, which means I only have $150 left on the card because the annual fee was charged at the start."

Grayson nodded his head. "Which means you'll max out that credit card on two dinner/appetizer/dessert combos at The Straight Wharf, and then you have to worry about tipping and ordering drinks. Sam, that doesn't sound like a great idea."

"Well, see, I could pay off that annual fee of $100, so I'll have $250 on the card to spend on dinner," Samantha said.

Grayson just shook his head. "Sam, that sounds like a terrible idea. Why don't you just invite him out for burgers at Lola's? That'll set you back around $50, and you won't even have to use that new credit card of yours."

"No, that won't do," Samantha said. "I need to impress

him. He knows I'm a cater waitress, but I don't want him to know I'm broke."

"Sam, obviously you're broke. You're a cater waitress on an island with a median household income of $110,000. It won't be a secret that you don't have a ton of money."

"Well, maybe I can make a cover story. You know, I'm really a trust fund baby, like him, but I was only working the event as a cater waitress because I was bored and wanted something to do. Or maybe I'm spying for another large corporation. Or something like that."

Grayson had to laugh. "Oh, really, Sam? You'd prefer the guy think you're a spy for a corporation instead of being honest and telling him you're dirt broke?"

"No," Samantha admitted. "I was hoping that my broke status would be a draw for him. You know, like in that book, *Fifty Shades of Grey*. She was a broke college student, and he was this like international billionaire self-made guy, and-"

"And he whipped her with a belt because that was how he got his rocks off," Grayson said. "No offense, Sam, but I think that finding a kinky billionaire who loves to inflict pain on you wouldn't be up your alley."

"Yeah, but there are other stories of other billionaires who don't like inflicting pain but really are looking for girls like me."

"If you say so," Grayson said. "But it seems like the jerk-wad alpha-holes who treat their women like dirt is the prevailing trope in the romance genre."

"But they only act that way because they're so emotionally scarred, and when they meet the woman they love, they become like big pussycats. I mean, Christian Grey was beaten by his mother's pimp and lay next to her body for four days, eating frozen peas to stay alive. And Ana's love saved him."

Grayson rolled his eyes. "You say they become pussycats, but pussy-whipped sounds more like it. And, news flash, jerks don't usually change, not even when they find the beautiful girl who is the only one for them. They're still jerks, and they're jerks to any woman who's unlucky enough to get sucked into their web. And anybody who has had as much trauma as Christian Grey had wouldn't just change into a nice guy because he falls in love."

He saw in Samantha's beautiful pixie face with the large blue eyes, button cute nose and bow-shaped lips that she was getting more and more disappointed with every word he said. It was obvious that the girl had it in her head that these romance novels were true. He'd read his share of these books himself because he liked to read widely. He was a writer, after all, and he had to read as much as he could to strengthen his own writing. But, unlike Samantha, he knew the romance novels were fantasies, just as much as his urban fantasy novels were.

Samantha had as much of a chance to snag herself a billionaire husband who treated her like gold as his urban fantasy heroine Alina had in saving the world on her own. Sure, maybe Samantha could catch the eye of a rich dude. She was beautiful and vivacious and sweet, like a butterfly. She had the kind of innocent quality that many men found to be catnip.

But if she did manage to snag a rich guy, the chances were that she was going to end up roadkill, ran over by the rich guy's Rolls Royce tires. Samantha was just too naïve not to get played by a rich guy who was up to no good.

"I suppose you're right," Samantha said with a sad look on her face. "I don't have what it takes to become the woman who tames the wealthy beast."

Grayson put his arm around Samantha and squeezed. "Now, now, don't be down on yourself. Hell, if anybody has what it takes to charm a wealthy dude into falling head over heels, it's you."

Samantha smiled wanly. "Thanks for saying that." Then she yawned. "I have to be at the bakery at noon, so I have to get a little sleep."

He smiled. "Are you going to be making any cakes for this bakery yet?"

She rolled her eyes. "I wish. You know, Cynthia has been the one they've been going to for the wedding cakes. She's such a hack. No creativity whatsoever. I just know I'd do a better job than her. I've shown my sketches to Javier, and he's impressed by them, but he doesn't want to give me the gig. I guess he thinks I need to learn more about the mechanics of making the cake, the flavors, the icing, all of that. But I know all that. He just won't give me a chance."

Grayson bit his tongue and said nothing. He wanted to remind her that he'd always encouraged her to enter culinary school. "You know, you have a passion for this. Or, at least, you have a great deal of interest in it, and your sketches are beautiful. If you just go to school, all the best bakeries will give you a chance. I think you'd really set the cake world on fire."

"Maybe." Then she yawned. "Listen, I'm exhausted. So help me to my bed?"

As he tucked her in, he thought about how much he wanted to join her in that bed. Not that he would ever tell her he was thinking that. But that was on his mind as he stayed awake for the rest of the early morning hours, typing away on his computer his fantasies featuring Samantha's doppelgänger Alina, the superhero diva who could save entire cities with her glowing hands, and her epic romance with Thorson, the nerd who loves her by day, and, by night, saves the city right alongside her.

CHAPTER 11

SAMANTHA

The day after Adrian brought Samantha home, after Grayson drove her to her car, she eagerly woke up and Facebook messaged him. She let him know how grateful she was that he'd saved her and brought her home. She also offered to buy him a drink and dinner at The Straight Wharf. It was always known to be crazy busy on the weekends, which was good for her because she looked forward to standing around with him in the waiting room and getting to know him.

However, he had a different idea. "I was hoping you would contact me because I wondered how you were. So, how are you?" He'd called her after she left her phone number through the Facebook message.

"I'm fine, thanks for asking. But I'd love to treat you to dinner. After all, you really did a nice thing for me in bringing me home the other night. The least I can do is treat you to a meal and drink."

"Actually, I can't let you buy me dinner. I'm sorry, I've seen where you live, and I hesitate to think you have the financial wherewithal to buy me dinner at a place like The Straight Wharf."

Samantha found his bluntness rude, but at the same time, he was right. She knew dinner for two at that restaurant would set her back a hundred and fifty dollars at least, and, at that moment, she couldn't swing it.

Then she got an idea. "Well, listen, you're right. And thank you for being considerate. But, I happen to know there's a great place on 'Sconset. An adorable bed-and-breakfast with quite a view. And, my mother owns it, so it won't be setting me back any."

She knew her mother probably wouldn't be too happy with her if she just showed up out of the blue with a guy in tow. She probably needed to go over there and ease her mother into the idea that she'd be bringing Adrian over there for a meal.

"Ok. You're on. When would you like to meet?"

"Give me a couple of days," Samantha said. She'd just go on over there and sweet talk her mother and then let her know about her plans.

Her mother wouldn't turn her down, and it helped that she was such a good cook. She could make her famous scallops casserole, and who knows? Adrian could help her drum up business.

Samantha hung up the phone and squealed. "He's going to go out with me!" She started to dance around the room. "Did you hear that, Grayson? A billionaire wants to go out with me. With me. Oh my God, what will I wear?"

Grayson was sitting on the couch, reading a book. He barely glanced up when Samantha started in with her hysterical gleeful shouting.

"Nice," Grayson said unenthusiastically.

"Come into my room, Grayson, help me find something to wear."

"I actually have a thing," Grayson said. "I have to go."

Samantha pouted. "A thing? What kind of a thing?"

"I'm, uh, going to the bookstore. An author is coming to sign some books and give a lecture on how he found his publisher. My writing group arranged it."

Grayson attended a weekly writing critique group that occasionally arranged for local authors to come in and give advice to the aspiring authors. But Samantha thought this particular event was next week.

"That's not today," Samantha said. "It's-"

"Yes, it's today," Grayson said, his words coming out quickly. Too quickly. Samantha knew he was lying but had no idea why he would be. "It's today. And I'm late. So, you're just going to have to find someone else to help you find the right outfit."

At that, Grayson closed his book, got his book bag and put his laptop into it and saluted Samantha. "Later," he said, and split.

Samantha looked out the window at Grayson, who was speeding out of their driveway. She wondered what had gotten into him. "Well," she said to herself with a shrug. "I guess I'm just going to have to hit somebody else up." Then she smiled. "I know! I'll take some outfits over to my mother's house, and I'll tell her about my plans to bring Adrian over, and she can critique my outfits. Two birds, one stone."

And, with a snap of her fingers, Samantha headed over to her mother's new house.

CHAPTER 12

AVA

Ava was busy, busy, busy these days with the running of her bed and breakfast. She was astounded at how well her place was doing. It was packed, night after night, and Ava could charge $500 per room instead of the $400 she was previously charging. That gave her some breathing room, financially-wise, at least. But it left her with barely time to breathe.

There was always something to tend to, and Ava had been doing it all, aside from the cooking of the meals. She cleaned every toilet spotlessly every single day, and made sure that each restroom was well-stocked with linens, toilet paper and Poo-Pouri, a product Ava couldn't live without, because it basically took the stink out of the bathrooms. She made all the beds and changed the sheets herself after the guests left. She assiduously dusted hard surfaces, mopped the hardwood floors and vacuumed the area rugs. She waited on the guests when they ate their meals, bussed the tables and did the dishes. She checked everybody in and out, and, when she had a moment between basic chores and checking in guests, she was hard at work on the computer, reviewing who was making reservations and who was on the waiting list.

Thank God Jessica was now there to help her! Jessica was proving to be a terrific asset, and a very hard worker. Ava found that the young lady really knew how to clean and was just as assiduous as Ava was. After Jessica cleaned a room, it would always pass the white-glove test, which was important to Ava.

And she had a waiting list! She never thought she could possibly be more thrilled in her life. To think, she wasted all those years knee-deep in legal jargon and representing billionaires who want to cheat Uncle Sam, when she could've been running her own bed and breakfast and having the time of her life!

She shuddered to think about the grind she left when she was fired from Collins and Lahy. No more opposing counsels undermining her, judges barking at her, partners chastising her and clients berating her. Now, all she saw were happy people, because they were on vacation, they were staying on the beach, and they were surrounded by luxury.

Just then, as Ava was busily checking in some new people, she looked up from her computer and saw Samantha coming through the door. "Hey, Sam," Ava said to her as she gave a young couple their room key and told them to have fun while they were staying with her. "What can I do for you?"

"Mom, I need to talk to you. I mean, now. I mean, it's an emergency." Her daughter's big blue eyes were frantic. Ava knew that look anywhere, as Samantha tended towards drama in her life. Everything was an emergency in Samantha's world.

Ava looked at her computer and saw there wasn't anybody due to arrive for another couple of hours and nodded her head. "You've come at a good time," she said. "The dining room is closed until dinnertime. Ordinarily, I would be using these hours between lunch and dinnertime to clean the rooms, but I can give my beautiful daughter a bit of my time instead. Besides, Jessica is here, and she's cleaning the rooms instead."

Ava wished Samantha would've taken her up on living there in exchange for her labor, just because she wanted to keep an eye on her. But she knew Samantha had other ideas, and she wanted to work someplace where she'd be able to meet eligible wealthy men.

What Ava wanted to tell her daughter was that billionaires weren't what they were billed as in the romance novels. At least the ones she represented at Collins and Lahy weren't. Her clients, aside from James Bloch, the wonderful man who was like her surrogate father and actually turned out to be her biological father, were universally pigs. They were greedy, selfish, pompous and most of them were just plain mean. They treated her like a servant, even though she'd graduated from Harvard Law School and had written winning Supreme Court briefs.

Ava didn't know if they treated her terribly because she was a woman or thought they were better than her. After all, they were masters of the universe, legends in their own minds, and she wasn't. She was just a lowly peon in the grand scheme of things, and they treated her accordingly.

No, Ava didn't want Samantha to land a rich guy because she knew her daughter wouldn't be happy with one. But there was little dissuading Sam when she got a thought into her head. Ava knew the best way to handle Samantha was to let whatever it was obsessing her to play itself out.

Ava and Samantha headed up to the deck and took a seat.

" Okay, now," Ava said, facing Samantha. "What's the big emergency?"

THE BEACHSIDE REUNION..

Samantha nodded her head. "Mom, you just won't believe it, but you have to believe it. I have a date with a billionaire." Then she squealed at the top of her lungs.

Ava cocked her head at her daughter. "A billionaire, huh? How did you meet said billionaire?"

"He's the son of Noah and Ellen Ripley."

"Okay," Ava said. "And am I supposed to know who Noah and Ellen Ripley are?"

"You should, mom. Everybody should know them. I mean, you've heard of Elon Musk, haven't you?"

"The Tesla guy," Ava said. "Yes, I'm aware of him." She was annoyed at Elon Musk because he seemed to be yet another billionaire who didn't want to pay taxes. However, he was better than her clients in that he paid *some* of his earnings to Uncle Sam. Not enough in Ava's estimation because for several years, he only paid around $70,000 in income taxes on a wealth of over $150 billion and didn't pay any tax at all in 2018. But still, aside from 2018, Musk's tax burden wasn't zero, and he came by his low tax bill legally. Which spoke volumes about how much the country needed to change its tax code, but that was another conversation for another time.

"Well, mom, then you know about how much money is in alternative energy. And Noah Ripley is really into that green technology, mom. He's the founder and the CEO of Greengenix, which has a huge government contract to help countries around the world build their clean energy infrastructure. So, he's saving the world."

"Sounds like a good guy," Ava said. "He devotes his resources for the betterment of earth. But you aren't going out with Noah, but his son. What's he like?"

"Well, he doesn't really have a job," Samantha said. "But that's the best part, mom. I mean, he has all the time in the world to travel, and you know it's always been my dream to see different countries. His father doesn't ever have time to do anything but work. He wasn't even at the ALS fundraiser because he was out of the country. I've done research on him and he's usually not in the United States, but in Europe and Asia, working all the time."

Ava raised an eyebrow. "Sam, I don't think I need to tell you that a man who has never worked a day in his life and lives off of somebody else is probably not somebody you want to date. I don't think you realize how privileged and entitled people act. Especially privileged and entitled men."

"Mom, come on. You sound prejudiced. I mean, Adrian literally saved my life the other night. I think that means he's not who you think he is."

"Oh, I think he probably is exactly who I think he is," Ava said. "Wait, what? What do you mean he literally saved your life?"

"I almost drowned, mom," Samantha said. "I got swept away with a big wave the other night, and he jumped right in and saved me."

Ava put her hand to her chest and felt her heart thumping. "Samantha, you are going to put me into an early grave. You have to stop taking so many stupid chances with your life."

"I am, mom, really. That was a rogue wave that got me. I was standing on the shore with my toes in the surf and that wave just came in and knocked me off my feet. It wasn't my fault. Honestly. Anyhow, my almost drowning was the greatest thing ever, because it brought me to Adrian."

Ava rolled her eyes but bit her tongue. "All right, Samantha, so you have a date with this Noah Ripley guy. What does that have to do with me?"

"It's not Noah, mom, it's Adrian. Noah is the father. Adrian is the son."

"Oh, okay, Adrian. You have a date with Adrian. I still don't know what this has to do with me." She had a bad feeling that Samantha would bring him to the inn and ask her to make them dinner because Samantha didn't have the money to take this guy out.

And Ava was absolutely sure that Samantha asked Adrian out, not the other way around. She knew her daughter well enough that she could always read her like a dinner menu.

"Well, mom, actually, I asked him out. I wanted to tell him' thank you for saving my life.' And, well, I can't really afford to take him someplace nice. So, I invited him to eat here. I want him to be impressed and see I have a successful mother, so maybe he'll think I'm successful, too."

"Oh, I see. You're successful-adjacent so that makes you also successful. That's what you're thinking?"

"Something like that. Successful-adjacent, I like that," Samantha said. "But yeah, mom, I wanted him to eat here with me."

Ava sighed. "Okay, Samantha, I'll make him dinner tonight. But I have several conditions."

Samantha was now jumping up and down and clapping her hands. "Thank you, thank you, thank you," she chanted.

"My conditions are number one, this is the first and last time you hit me up for a free meal with Adrian. Number two, you eat what I fix. Don't worry, I was going to make scallops casserole and chocolate lava cake, so it should be a hit."

Samantha nodded her head rapidly up and down. "Oh, yes, your scallops casserole is the best. I'm sure he'll love it! And your chocolate lava cake is divine, mom."

"Good. Because I don't want to treat the two of you like you're guests who are dining here because it'll mess with my inventory. Plus, Reilly and his crew have enough on their plates making food for the guests every day. So, I'll be making the food for you and this Adrian. You have to tell him he won't have a choice in his meal. He might not like that."

"Oh, I'm sure he'll be fine," Samantha said. "Who doesn't love scallops casserole?"

"Okay. Well, then, what time can I expect the two of you? I'm going to reserve the deck." It was necessary to reserve the deck because every evening, people headed up to the deck to have a glass of wine or to lounge in the hot tub or to just look over the railing at the raging surf below.

"How about 8?" Samantha asked.

"8 it is," Ava said. "But are you sure you want to do it tonight? Doesn't that seem a little rushed?"

"I managed to reel him in, mom, and if I don't land him tonight, he might get away. Like a fish. You have to act fast, or that fish is going to swim off."

"Dear," Ava said. "If he's the right guy, he's not going to swim off. I'll be happy to host you guys here tonight, but you should probably think twice about chasing after a guy who you're afraid will get off the hook if you don't act immediately."

"Noted," Samantha said, giving her mother a hug. "Now, I brought over some outfits, and I'm going to model them for you. You can tell me which one I should go with. Grayson was supposed to do this, but he bailed on me with some lame excuse about his writing group inviting an author to give a lecture." Samantha rolled his eyes. "He's a big liar. He just doesn't want to help me out, for some reason."

Ava had a pretty good idea what that reason was. She always felt Grayson was in love with her daughter - it was just how he always looked at her - but Samantha seemed blind to this fact. And Ava wasn't going to butt in. If Grayson wanted to tell Samantha about his feelings, then he would. Until then, it wasn't up to Ava to get her daughter to open her eyes.

For her part, Ava always hoped Samantha *would* open her eyes. Grayson, broke as he was, would be a catch in Ava's eyes. He'd be somebody who would always treat her like gold, which was all Ava wanted for her children. All of them.

"Well, let me get the girls over here," Ava said. "If they're available at the moment, they can come on over and give you their input, too."

"That would be fun, mom," Samantha said enthusiastically. "Go ahead, see if they're available."

Ava thought her friends probably wouldn't be able to come over, because Hallie was so busy getting the new spa up and running and Quinn was busy with her interior decorating business and with raising her new daughter.

Fortunately, she was wrong. Both Quinn and Hallie were available to come over, as Quinn was working from home that day and Hallie was as well, because she was working on the spa's social media pages. Sarah, however, couldn't be there, because she was in California, finalizing a contract from a winery out in Napa.

Although both women were busy working from home, they agreed to come over because they needed a bit of a break. "And sugar, just between you and me, Emerson is driving me up a tree. I think I have to leave the house right now, because if I don't, I going to wring her beautiful little neck," Quinn said.

"That bad, huh?" Ava asked, feeling for her friend. She'd been to that dark place where the kids seemed out of control, and she was at her wits' end. She was convinced that one of her triplets would end up dead in a ditch somewhere just because she was a catastrophizer and her mind went to the worse-case scenario in an embarrassingly short period of time. Thus far, her triplets were all good kids, even if she did worry that Samantha was aimless, Charlotte was stressed and Jackson was in a dog-eat-dog profession that tended to eat people up and spit them out. But they weren't on drugs, they weren't alcoholic, and they didn't cause Ava too many heartaches. She was lucky that way.

"Oh, sugar, I don't want to talk about it. It's not as bad as it was, of course, but let's just say that girl is too smart for her own good. I'm so looking forward to next week, when I put her into a music camp for the next couple of months. For now, I just want to see pretty little Samantha modeling pretty little clothes for an hour or so. We'll be over within a half-hour."

Quinn had found a high-dollar camp for Emerson to attend. It was a camp for musical prodigies like Emerson. It was a two-month intensive boot camp for gifted musicians. Emerson was looking forward to it, almost jumping out of her skin in anticipation of it. Ava would miss her playing with Deacon on Friday and Saturday nights, but it couldn't be helped. She was just happy the girl had something to look forward to.

Quinn and Hallie were good as their word, and they arrived at Ava's home in twenty minutes. "Well, come on, girl, let's see those gorgeous legs," Quinn teased Samantha as Sam went into the bathroom to change. Ava poured her and Hallie some mimosas, and the ladies sat in their loungers and listened to the ocean waves and sounds of beach action while they waited for Samantha to re-emerge in outfit number 1.

For the next hour or so, Quinn, Hallie and Ava drank mimosas and watched Samantha model one outfit after another. Since most of her outfits seemed to show too much skin, the three women finally helped her choose a little black dress that wasn't plunging and had a fringed skirt. It showed off her best assets - her square shoulders and curvy hips - without giving too much away.

"And pearls," Ava said, slurring her words ever-so-slightly.

She was getting buzzed off the mimosas, so she knew that she had to cut herself off.

Samantha excitedly nodded her head and hugged Ava. "Thanks, mom, for helping me with this."

"Of course. I'll be seeing you tonight."

CHAPTER 13

AVA

That evening, Ava hosted Samantha and Adrian at the house. Her specialty was scallops casserole. First, she made the topping. She crushed up some Ritz crackers and combined them with salted butter, parmesan cheese and paprika. She combined fresh scallops, more butter, sherry, flour, half and half, and eggs for the filling. She carefully cooked the filling and then poured it into a casserole dish and topped it with the crackers. Then she baked it for 20 minutes.

She also made a fresh Caprese salad with some heirloom tomatoes that she'd picked up at the Farmer's Market that day. She combined the tomatoes with some fresh basil and buffalo mozzarella from an Italian deli in town. A bottle of buttery Chardonnay, oak-aged with hints of grapefruit, orange and lime, was chilling on ice.

For dessert, Ava prepared a chocolate raspberry lava cake. She melted butter and high-quality dark chocolate and mixed it with sugar, eggs and flour. Then she mashed up fresh raspberries she found at the Farmer's Market and combined them with raspberry preserves. She layered the chocolate concoction with the raspberry mix and baked it for 15 minutes.

She loved this dessert - the chocolate cake was moist, sugary, and decadent. The fruit middle was puckery yet sticky sweet. She loved dipping her fork into the cake and seeing the raspberry filling ooze out.

Ava had an absolute ball shopping for this meal. She went to the Glidden's Island Seafood market for the scallops, which was on the water and housed in a Cape Cod wood-shingled home. The place had been around for over 120 years and offered all manner of fresh catch seafood.

It was a glorious day, and Ava couldn't help but feel amazed she could ride her bike to the market, and she was thrilled that she actually could get away from the inn, because Jessica was doing so well helping out. The market was seven miles away from where she lived, and there were bike paths everywhere. Ava took an insulated backpack cooler that kept the food fresh, so she could buy all she needed for the meal while enjoying a gorgeous late-June day.

The overall charm of the island made Ava feel more alive than she'd felt in a long time. She loved to see people picnicking in various parks, to smell the ocean air, to ride over the cobble-stone streets. The historical buildings piqued her curiosity as she imagined wealthy Bostonians from days gone by living in these mansions. She could also envision lonely women standing on their roof decks, watching for their husbands to come home from the sea.

She sang songs to herself as she went from the fish market, picking up the fresh scallops and a filet of cod for the next night's meal, to the Italian deli for the fresh mozzarella. And then over to the Farmer's Market, where there was all manner of fresh vegetables and fruit, beautiful produce representing all colors of the rainbow. She picked only the ripest tomatoes, only the freshest scallops, fish and cheese.

When she got back to 'Sconset, she stopped by the Old Historic District. This area was marked by a quiet cobble-stoned street lined with shops housed in Cape Cod wood-shingled buildings, interspersed with Colonial-style brick structures. The 'Sconset market was in one of the wood-shingled buildings. Ava could pick up some other kinds of cheese, eggs, butter, cream, condiments, bread and preserves. She also picked up some dark chocolate baking bars, sugar and flour for her famous chocolate lava cake.

By this time, her backpack was stuffed, so it was time to head back and start the meal. When she got back, she invited the girls over. Quinn and Hallie both came over and popped open a bottle of wine Ava had picked up at the Nantucket Vineyard, the local winery. The three women set out to make up the meal together.

Hallie chopped veggies for the salad while Quinn was busy melting the chocolate and butter and mashing up the raspberries. Ava worked on making the casserole. While they worked, they listened to music and caught up on what they were doing.

"Oh, sugar," Quinn said as she made the cake. "I sure hope this guy is worth all this trouble."

"I doubt he is," Ava said. "Knowing Sam. What I wouldn't give for her guest to be Grayson. I don't know when Sam's going to wake up about him. I only hope it happens soon because Grayson is a catch."

"Oh, but your daughter has stars in her eyes about a rich guy sweeping her off her feet," Hallie said as she chopped the tomatoes, tore the basil and sliced the cheese. "Just like Cinderella. Do you know how much damage that fairy tale has done? Everybody thinks Prince Charming is going to show up. And then maybe he does. But nobody ever told

Cinderella that Prince Charming will leave his socks on the floor for weeks on end, will work so much that she doesn't see him and will have moods that put the wicked step-sisters to shame. I think somebody needs to revise that fairy tale to show what happens after the happily ever after."

"Yes, Samantha is looking for a rich guy," Ava said as she laughed about Hallie's characterization of Cinderella. It was *so* true. "Because she doesn't know what direction to turn in her life."

Quinn just raised an eyebrow. "Well, I took the time to do a Google search on this guy Adrian. He's financially sound, but there are pictures online of him with different women all the time. He dates New York models and actresses, and celebrities who summer on the island. I don't know, Ava. He seems like a womanizer."

"That's what I was afraid of," Ava said. "Well, I'll set up a candlelight dinner for them on the deck, after which I'll join them for a nightcap and try to grill him as much as I can."

Ava put the casserole and the cake into their respective ovens. Then she went out to the deck and put a white tablecloth on one of the tables, along with some freshly-cut flowers in a vase, and lit a candle. She also placed two heat lamps right by the table, as it was a chilly night. It was almost 7, so the sun was going down. Sam and Adrian were going to be there at 7:30. Ava hoped she timed everything okay.

At 7:30, Sam arrived, looking beautiful in her basic black dress and peep-toe fire-engine red heels. Like Ava had suggested, she paired the dress with a choker of pearls, and her blonde hair was piled up on her head.

She beamed when she saw the deck.

"Oh, mom," Sam said, looking around the deck. In addition to the table cloth, candle and flowers, Ava also took the time to string white lights around the deck. The ocean was rolling in, the stars were coming out, and the moon was full.

"This is beautiful. Thank you for doing this." Sam gave Ava a huge hug.

Ava had actually taken the time to reserve the entire deck for Sam and Adrian, just for the evening. Her guests were a little disappointed they couldn't go to the deck that evening, but Ava personally assured all of them that they could have full use of the deck starting the next day.

Ava just smiled.

Samantha sat down, looking around the deck with awe. "I mean, this deck was beautiful in the daytime. But at night, it's spectacular. This is better than any restaurant I could take this guy to."

Adrian arrived at 8:00. He didn't apologize for being late, which Ava noted. She also thought the body language the guy exhibited showed he wasn't that into her daughter. He hugged Sam stiffly when he got to the deck, and then, just as stiffly, he turned to Ava and awkwardly shook her hand.

Ava had a sinking feeling as she watched Sam eagerly sit down and start talking in a bubbly manner to Adrian, who sat as stiffly as a stone.

"Oh my God, do you believe this place, Adrian? I admit, when I found out my mom was opening up a place here on the island, I wasn't expecting much, but this house is so gorgeous, and this deck! I mean..." She shook her head and took a sip of the wine that Ava had placed on the table.

"Yes, it's nice," Adrian said without enthusiasm. Ava rolled her eyes as she placed some rolls and butter on the table, along with the Caprese salad. She planned to keep an eye on the two as she served them and bussed the table.

"And it's such a beautiful view, too. You can see the ocean from here, and you can smell the saltwater and hear the waves. Sometimes I have to pinch myself. I feel so lucky to be living on this island. I mean, there are millions of stars in the sky. When I lived in New York, there were like a fraction of the stars."

"Actually, there are the exact same amount of stars on this island as in New York," Adrian said. "Sorry, but that's a pet peeve of mine. People who act like there are more stars in the country than in the city. As if the universe contracts and expands like that."

Samantha didn't notice that Adrian just put her in her place for something perfectly innocent. Most people talked about the stars on Nantucket compared to the city. Leave it to Adrian to get all technical about Samantha's charming observation.

"Well, you know what I mean," Samantha said. "You can just see more stars here than in New York. And pretty soon, it's going to be time to catch fireflies. I absolutely love fireflies, don't you?"

"Sure," Adrian said. "I guess so."

Ava left the two "love birds" and went to get the main course, the scallops casserole. Quinn and Hallie were in the kitchen, still drinking wine, and Ava took a sip of her own glass of wine as she headed towards the oven.

"Well, it's going swimmingly up there," Ava said, sarcasm dripping from her voice.

"That good?" Quinn asked.

"Yeah," Ava said. "It's like trying to watch a butterfly flirt with a stone. I have a feeling that Sam picked another dud."

Quinn put her arm around Ava. "She'll figure it out, sugar. In the meantime, you just have to support her and hope she comes to her senses sooner rather than later."

Ava shook her head and headed back up to the deck, her scallops casserole in her hands. She sliced some up for her daughter and Adrian, then removed the salad plates.

She noticed Samantha was still talking, and Adrian wasn't making eye contact with her. He was staring into the distance as Samantha told him all about what she wanted to do with her life.

"I'm working at a bakery and cater waitress, and in my spare time, I'm going to drive Uber, as soon as I get another car. But my dream is to be a cake decorator here on the island. And with all the weddings this island hosts, I could really stay busy doing that type of thing. I know I have it in me to do a great job with that. I just have to get the courage to try."

"That's nice," Adrian said and then took another sip of wine. "Does your mom stock any hard alcohol? I could really use a harder drink."

"I think she does," Sam said, looking at Ava. "Mom, you got some hard stuff, didn't you?"

"Of course," Ava said. She had vodka, whiskey, gin and tequila, along with some bitters and mixers. She also had cherries and citrus fruits for garnishing. "What would you like, Adrian?"

"Can you make an Old Fashioned?" Adrian asked her.

"One Old Fashioned, coming up," Ava said, saluting the guy.

Then she went into the kitchen and found the bitters and a bottle of Bulleit whiskey. She muddled the bitters with water and sugar and put that into a glass. On top of that, she added the whiskey and lemon peel. She garnished the glass with an orange slice and then took it out to Adrian.

Adrian nodded his head when Ava appeared with the cocktail. "Thanks," he said.

"Mom, this casserole is absolutely divine," Sam said. "This is next level, mom. You've really outdone yourself."

"Well, it helps that the scallops are so fresh," Ava said. "I always made this casserole with previously frozen scallops before because that's all I could find in New York."

"Well, whatever, the flavors in this thing just sing. The

sherry, butter and cream, cheese, and crackers all just go with the scallops. I don't think I've ever tasted anything so rich, decadent and just yummy."

Ava beamed and then looked at Adrian. He was sipping his drink and didn't tell Ava what he thought about the food. Nor did he compliment her on the drink she made. She personally thought the drink was delicious, as she put a little of it into a shot glass as a taster.

"Just wait until I bring out the dessert," Ava said. "Chocolate raspberry lava cake."

Sam's eyes got wide when Ava mentioned the dessert. "Oh, mom, you remembered how much I love chocolate and raspberries." Then she looked at Adrian. "I just can't wait to make a groom's cake or even a bride's cake with chocolate and fruit. We're talking ganache and blood oranges. You just won't taste anything better. Blood orange buttercream, blood orange filling and dark chocolate. Swoon."

"Um, no dessert for me," Adrian said, putting his hands up. Then he looked at his watch. "I have an early meeting tomorrow, so I really should be getting home. It's getting late."

"Late?" Samantha said. "It's only 9:30."

"Well, I have a thing tomorrow morning. I'll, uh, show myself out."

At that, he shook Ava's hand and disappeared down the stairs that led to the street. Sam was left at the table, her mouth agape.

"What just happened?" Sam asked.

Ava took a deep breath. "Well, he has a thing in the morning. I guess he just needed to get home and get some shut-eye." Samantha knew Adrian had just given her the bum's rush. There was no way around it.

Sam just looked stunned. "Mom, tomorrow's Sunday."

"Well, maybe you know, maybe his thing is a meeting

with his father about something. You know how upset I get when I schedule a time to see you kids and you're late. It might be as simple as that."

"But mom, he never said before he had to be up tomorrow morning. And he didn't even tell me why he has to be up in the morning." She shook her head and stared at the sky. "I don't believe it. You went all out, and I really took a long time getting ready. And-"

Sam started to cry, and Ava's heart went out to her. "Tell you what," Ava said. "I have this beautiful cake all ready to go. It would be such a shame for it to go to waste. Quinn and Hallie are here and would love to share this cake with you. And we can call Grayson to join us."

Samantha just nodded her head. "Okay. That sounds fun. I mean, we can't let that cake go to waste."

Samantha called Grayson, who agreed to come over. Since Grayson and Samantha's house was within walking distance of Ava's place, he was at the house in 15 minutes.

Grayson made a bee-line for Samantha and sat next to her.

"Oh, Grayson," Samantha said to her best friend. "I really thought this was going to happen with Adrian and me. I don't know what went wrong."

"Maybe nothing went wrong," Grayson said. "Maybe he just really needed to get up in the morning."

"Maybe," Samantha said. "Anyhow, my mom's friends are going to be out here. My mom's going to build a fire in that pit and serve some cake. I'm happy you're here."

Grayson smiled and then looked up in the sky. "I can never get over how many stars there are out here," he said.

Ava grinned and shook her head. She got the cake. Quinn and Hallie joined Grayson and Samantha in eating it.

"Ava," Grayson said as he took a bite of the chocolate-raspberry concoction. "This is probably the most delicious cake I've ever had, and I mean ever. How do you do it?"

"Lots of butter and sugar," Ava said. "And the best chocolate and raspberries I could find. Imported chocolate from Brussels, raspberries from the Farmer's Market. You get quality ingredients, and you get a quality cake."

"Well, however you made it, I salute you."

Ava thought about Grayson's enthusiastic reaction to her food and Adrian's non-reaction and thought again about how foolish Samantha was for not looking Grayson's way.

There was a chill in the air, and Ava gave Samantha and Grayson a blanket. After the dessert, they went over to the love seat and put the blanket over them. Sam put her head on Grayson's shoulder, and Grayson put his head on hers. There was another bottle of wine on the table in front of them. They were pouring the wine into glasses and sipping.

Ava left them there. "Just let yourself out," Ava told her daughter. "When you're done. I'm going to bed." The others had already gone inside, and Ava was tired and ready for bed.

"'Night, mom," Samantha said.

"'Night, Ava," Grayson said.

"Good night."

As Ava went inside, she felt terrible for her daughter because Samantha was so excited about Adrian, who evidently turned out to be a dud.

At the same time, she saw how easy Samantha and Grayson were together and said a little prayer that her daughter would open her damn eyes.

CHAPTER 14

After Andrew came to stay at the 'Sconset Inn, Jessica knew she'd have to get up to speed on his music. Ava and her friends obviously knew all about him before he ever stepped foot in the house, and Jessica only knew him from the article she read in the *Rolling Stone*. So she immersed herself in his music, and reveled in the lyrics and the harmonies he was able to put together. His music definitely was deep. It was all about first loves and familial ties and the bonds that people have with one another.

She and Andrew were becoming good friends, which really helped her immensely. She found she did not even think about OxyContin when she was in his presence. And, because he was trying to keep a low profile, he was usually around the house. Jessica, of course, was busy all the time, because the 'Sconset Inn was constantly filled to capacity. All the bedrooms were full, every day of the week.

As for her job, she did everything around the house, wherever she was needed – laundry, cleaning the bathrooms, mopping up the floors, vacuuming, chopping vegetables in the kitchen, taking reservations. Wherever she was needed, she cheerfully chipped in.

Just about every evening, Andrew invited her to go down to the beach with him. They couldn't hang out on the deck, because the deck was always filled with people in the hot tub and around the various fire rings. The beach was more deserted, at least it was in the evenings. By 8 o'clock, the darkness had settled, and while there were a few people here and there walking along the shore, or sitting around bonfires, Andrew and Jessica were able to stake out a small plot all for themselves. Andrew explained he really liked her feedback on his music, and she loved giving it.

Because they were becoming such good friends, Andrew offered to share his book of poetry with her. "You talked about how people who have darkness in their life usually put that darkness into their art? And I told you the reason why I find the light in my music is because that's what I need? Do you remember that conversation?"

Of course, Jessica remembered that conversation. That was one of the first talks that she had had with him. "Yes."

He nodded his head. "Well, let's just say that my newer songs might be optimistic and bright. But my poetry is not. If you really want to get a look into how I really feel, maybe you can read through them."

Jessica was thrilled. She had spotted the poetry book when she was cleaning his room. But she dared not look through it. She would no more look through that poetry book than she would open somebody's diary or journal without asking them. But she was intensely curious about it. Now, here Andrew was, offering this to her.

To say she felt very privileged to be offered this chance would be understating things.

So, Andrew gave her the book of poetry, and, one night after he had gone to bed, as did everybody else around her,

Jessica read. And he was right about that. The poetry was so different from his music. She could sense heartbreak, anguish, and a sense of bewilderment. There wasn't really anger, necessarily. But she could sense that somehow or another, he was very lost. And he, like her, was trying to piece together a tragedy that had happened when he was very young.

Somehow, as she read some of the deeper poems, she could piece the puzzle together about what happened to him very well. Somebody had threatened his life as a very young child. That much was clear. The words that jumped out at her were the words of somebody who had gone through a near-death experience at an age before he could process it, and yet it was burned in his brain. It was burned so clearly through his psyche that there was nothing he could do to get rid of these demons. She identified with this so clearly, yet she was envious that he could process it somehow. It was almost as if he knew exactly what happened to him, and she didn't. Yet, at the same time, she knew their experiences were very, very similar.

She felt tears in her eyes and a hole in her heart. She looked at the clock and saw it was 2 o'clock in the morning. Yet, she felt the burning need to speak with Andrew. Right at that very second, and not a moment later.

She tiptoed over to his bedroom and knocked on the door. He didn't answer, so she cracked open the door. He was sound asleep and snoring. She shook her head, knowing she had to talk to him. "Andrew," she said.

He stirred a little. "Jessica? What time is it?"

" 2 AM. I'm so sorry to be bothering you, but I was reading through your poems, and I have to talk to you."

He nodded his head. "Sure. I mean, if it's 2 o'clock in the morning and you're in here, obviously it's something you have to get off your chest right now."

She sat down in the big leather chair that was next to the bed. "Something happened to you. What? What is it that has fueled these poems?"

He sat up in the bed. "Yes. Something did happen to me. It's not something I talk about to anybody. I don't quite know why I don't talk about it to anybody. I guess because I feel so guilty about it. It's a reason why nobody has ever seen these poems besides myself, at least until now."

Jessica put her hand on the side of the chair. For some odd reason, she was bracing herself, hard. "Go ahead. What happened?"

He took a deep breath. "I remember this like it happened yesterday, but it happened when I was five years old. I was at a birthday party. At a park."

Jessica nodded her head.

"Yes. I was at a birthday party. For my best friend…"

Jessica took a deep breath. She shook her head. "I'm so sorry. I'm sorry to bother you. I don't know what I thought when I came in here. I'm so sorry."

Andrew didn't say anything more about the story. Jessica was grateful for that. Somehow she knew what he was going to tell her was the key to her own pain.

But she also knew she was not quite ready to unlock it just yet.

CHAPTER 15

ANDREW

That night Andrew had a dream. It was a dream he used to have on a regular basis, but, lately, he hadn't had the dream.

He was a young boy in his dream, probably about five years old. He was in a pair of swim trunks on a beach. He was running next to his little girlfriend, a blonde cherub by the name of Natalie. It must've been close to the 4th of July because Natalie was dressed in a red, white and blue one-piece swimsuit. Natalie had chubby legs and arms, and he was a string bean.

"Come on, Natalie, let's make a sandcastle!" he said to the young girl as they ran along the beach.

"No, I need to go in the water. Let's go in the water. Last one in is a rotten egg!"

The two raced to the water, and Natalie dove in headfirst. Natalie was a great swimmer. It was almost as if she was meant to be in the water, Andrew thought. She seemed like a mermaid out there, diving and bobbing, her strong arms and legs paddling furiously through the sea. Andrew wouldn't be surprised if she grew a tail, just like the mermaids he knew about from watching cartoons.

Andrew wanted to join her, but he wasn't nearly as good of a swimmer as her, and he didn't want to slow her down. So, he just stood by the shore, letting the water lap around his ankles. He saw some interesting seashells in the water, and he picked them up and put them in his pocket. He watched his friend continue to swim out in the deeper water, and he felt cowardly for not going out there with her. But he didn't feel confident he could get out in the deep part of the ocean and come back alive. So, he just didn't bother.

It seemed like she would never come in, so Andrew lost interest and went to the sand and started to build a castle. Somebody had a boom box, and, as usual, when he heard the music, he perked up. Music fed his soul, which was important because his father made his life miserable.

His mom explained that his father was still fighting a war in his head. His dad was a veteran of the Gulf War, and even though Andrew never knew him when he was fighting that war, he felt for his father. His dad was twitchy – whenever he heard loud noises of any sort, he would jump out of his skin. Andrew's bedroom was close to his parents, and he would hear his father screaming at night, just about every night. And sometimes, his father would get a look in his eye. He would just space out as if he saw something that wasn't there.

He didn't understand why his father was so strange. She heard his mother talk about something called PTSD, whatever that meant. His father saw a therapist about this PTSD thing, but Andrew wondered if it was doing any good. From the looks of things, it wasn't.

He wished he could be like his friend Natalie. He watched her still frolicking in the water, and it seemed she didn't have a care in the world. As far as he knew, she didn't. She seemed happy, bubbly, all the time. She giggled a lot, talked a lot, and he adored her. She was definitely his best friend.

Natalie finally came in from the water. "Why don't you go out there and join me?" she asked. "The water is so warm."

Andrew just shook his head. "I don't like to swim." Truth be told, he didn't really want to leave this part of the beach because the group of kids with the boombox were playing some music he really enjoyed. He felt his soul start to fly when he heard music that spoke to him. Maybe Natalie felt at home in the water, but he felt at home on the land, as long as there was music around.

Natalie stuck out her lower lip. "How do you know you don't like to swim? You never do it. You never even try to do it."

"I just know, that's all."

Natalie sat on the sand. "What you doing?" she asked him.

"What does it look like I'm doing? I'm making a sandcastle, silly."

"Can I help?"

"Sure."

"Just a second." Then she ran over to her mother, who was sitting on a blanket, a big floppy hat on her head. Natalie dug into a bag, and brought out two Barbie dolls and a Ken doll.

Then she came back over. "Here. These are my Barbies and my Ken. They want to live in the sandcastle. I hope there's room for them."

Andrew just scrunched up his nose. "They don't live in a castle. Don't they have like a townhouse or something?" Andrew remembered seeing a commercial for the Barbie townhouse. It was pink, which told him all he needed to know about that little townhouse. It certainly wasn't his style. And it also told him that Barbies didn't belong in a castle, whether it was made of sand or was real. Barbies belonged in a modern pink townhouse, and they drove modern pink cars.

He didn't know much about Barbies except that wherever they went, a trail of pink things followed them.

"That's not fair!" Natalie said, stomping her little foot. "They want to live in your sandcastle. They told me they wanted to live there, so you better let them live there."

Andrew looked at his sandcastle and wondered how two Barbies and a Ken would be happy in a little house like this. "By the way, there are two Barbies and only one Ken. How does that work?"

Natalie shook both of her Barbies in one hand and her Ken in the other. "I have 18 Barbies at home and only one Ken. They're all just really good friends. I'd have more than one Ken, but I really don't want another one. One's enough for me."

The Ken Natalie had was the one with yellow hair and suntan. There was another one on the market who had dark hair and no tan. "I think you need another Ken. Just one more. Your Ken with the yellow hair needs a boy buddy. He has enough girl buddies. He needs a boy to have as a friend."

"Okay. I'd like another one, but my mom tells me I have enough dollies. Now, can they live in your house?"

"Yes. They can."

And the next week, when Andrew and Natalie went to the beach, Andrew gave her a brand-new Ken doll. This new Ken doll was the one with the dark hair. "Now you have another one," Andrew said to his friend.

"Now I have another one," Natalie repeated. "I love you."

"I love you." And then he kissed her on her cheek. She turned red and giggled when he did that.

"What was that for?"

"Because that's what boys do when they love a girl. They kiss her on the cheek."

"Oh, okay."

And then she kissed him on the cheek. "Do girls kiss boys on the cheek too?" she asked.

" I guess so."

Andrew woke up, and wondered why he was having this dream again. He hadn't seen Natalie in so many years. In fact, he couldn't remember the last time he'd seen her. He did know that he didn't have any memories of Natalie after the age of five or six. That was probably because that was when he moved to Florida with his mother.

He wished he could close his eyes and think about the last time he saw his little friend, but he couldn't picture it. It was as if that little girl was a figment of his imagination, but he knew she wasn't. She was real. He knew her once. She was flesh and blood, as much flesh and blood as his own mother.

Why was he having this dream again? That was the real question in his mind. Maybe it was because he was back on Nantucket Island after so many years of being away. The dream he had of him and this little girl took place on this very island, on one of the beaches, but he couldn't remember which one.

That was it. That was the reason why he was having this dream.

That was the only reason why he was having this dream.

CHAPTER 16

SAMANTHA

Samantha had to add a restaurant job to make ends meet, so she applied and got a job at CRU, an elegant restaurant on Nantucket Harbor that afforded her a view of the yachts coming in every day. The place was an upscale seafood restaurant where the main courses started at $40 for the lobster roll and went up to $145 for a prime New York strip for two. Since the tickets were so large, Samantha made decent money at the place, even though she only worked there two evenings per week.

It had been a week since she and Adrian had dinner at her mother's house, and she hadn't heard from him since. Not that that was so surprising because, after all, he did leave the dinner in such a hurried fashion. Still, it was heartbreaking for Samantha. It seemed her dream of marrying a rich guy was in her grasp. Then, just as quickly, it was gone.

So, it was more than surprising when Adrian showed up at the restaurant one evening with a group of friends. All of them looked almost identical in Samantha's eyes. All were wearing casual but perfectly tailored suit jackets over their non-fussy button-downs, and khaki tailored pants hung perfectly over their leather boat shoes. All had hair worn high on the top, short on the sides, in various shades of blonde, brunette and red. All had perfect teeth and skin, as if they spent most of their lives in teeth-whitening trays and in various spas where they got regular facials.

Samantha's heart pounded when she saw Adrian, and was more than thrilled that she was the one who would be waiting on him. With shaking hands, she went over to the table. She felt her cheeks, and they were extremely warm.

"Hello," she said, her voice shaking. "My name is Samantha, and I'll be your server."

Adrian cocked his head at her and grinned. "Wait, you work here, too? Guys, this is Samantha, the girl I pulled out of the water the other night."

Samantha looked at the guys. "Yes, that's right, he saved my life."

One of the guys with dark hair nodded his head at Samantha. "Yeah, Adrian was telling us about what happened. Those rip tides are scary as hell, I'll tell you what. Especially when there's no lifeguard on duty. You better be careful. Those rogue waves can take you faster than you can say help!"

Adrian smiled at Samantha. "Well, Sam, why don't you get me a neat scotch," he said. And then Sam took drink orders around the table, and went to the bar to get everything.

She brought the guys their drinks and then took food and appetizer orders before turning her attention to other tables that were being sat in her section.

At some point, after she'd served Adrian several more neat scotches, but before the food was ready to serve, Adrian cornered Samantha as she was heading back to the kitchen to get some meals for a different table.

"Sam," he said. "I wanted to apologize for the other evening. The night I came over for dinner, I wasn't in the best of moods. I was tired and a bit hungover from the previous night and I had a fight with my dad early on in the day. I really acted like a jerk, and I just wanted to say I'm sorry."

Samantha's heart soared with every word. "Oh, it's really not a problem. I mean, everybody has bad days, you know. I have bad days, too."

He nodded his head. "Okay. Well, how are you? Have you been swept out by any more rogue waves?"

"No, I haven't really been to the beach since that night. I guess I'm a little afraid it might happen again, and you won't be around to save me."

He smiled. "Hey, I understand. But what do you say we give it another shot? Have dinner with me tomorrow night?"

Samantha's heart started to pound wildly out of her chest. Was this really happening? Was this Adrian really asking her out on a date?

"Um, yes, I don't have anything going on tomorrow night." *Well, aside from the fact that I'm scheduled to work. But I can trade shifts with Sheryl. She owes me.* Sheryl Woodson was another waitress at the CRU. Samantha had already traded shifts with her because she had to take her infant daughter to the ER. Sheryl told Samantha that, anytime she needed to trade shifts, she would be willing.

Adrian smiled again. "Meet you at Lola 41 tomorrow night at seven? I'm in the mood for some sushi. I hope you like sushi too. I think they have the best on the island."

Samantha felt like she was living in a dream. She was going to finally get her fairytale. She could just feel it. It was just a matter of time before she would be traveling around the world on a yacht. She could see herself in her mind's eye, sipping champagne on the deck of a 40-footer, feeling the breeze in her hair and having not a care in the world.

"I'll meet you there."

Adrian smiled and put his hand on Samantha's shoulder. "Good. I'll see you then."

And then he took his seat with the rest of his friends. Samantha continued to wait on him and his friends, bringing them their food and drinks, and feeling like she was floating on air the entire time. They left a good tip – two hundred dollars on a tab that ended up being a thousand. The bill was so high because they kept drinking long after their meals and desserts were finished, and, at some point, a group of women joined them for even more drinks. They closed down the restaurant, and they were there after Samantha had gotten off her shift. She still had to tend to them, even though she was technically off the clock. Or, at least she was supposed to have been off the clock at that point.

*****

After she got home, she tried to find Grayson. She was dying to tell him the news about her date. But, when she got home, he wasn't there. It was 1 o'clock in the morning, and she couldn't find him anywhere.

She went to look at the main house to see if there were any lights on, and she saw that Del was apparently still awake, because his office light was ablaze. She had been given a key to the main house, so she used it and knocked on Del's office door.

"Come in," Del's cheerful voice commanded her.

Sam walked into Del's office. "Do you know where Grayson is? I just got home from work, and he's not around."

Del chuckled a little. "I think he might have hooked up with somebody tonight. I saw him leaving the house around seven. Why? Are you jealous?"

Samantha shook her head. "No, not jealous. I just had some news I was dying to tell him about. I mean, I'm bursting at the seams here. I was just hoping he'd be around to hear it."

"Oh? What's your news?"

"Well, I have a date with a billionaire tomorrow night. I'm meeting him at Lola's. I guess we're going to get some sushi. And I'm bouncing off the walls."

"Well, congratulations. Who's the lucky fella?"

"Adrian Ripley."

"Noah Ripley's boy?"

"Yeah. You know of him?"

"It's a small island, and everybody kinda hears about the fat cats who live here. And Noah Ripley is one of the fattest cats around. He's such a fat cat that he's not eating Meow Mix. He's eating Tuna Tartar. I don't know much about his son, though. What does he do for a living?"

"He's a trust fund baby."

"Ah. Must be nice. Just kidding. I think if I were a trust fund baby, I'd be so bored I'd want to crawl out of my skull. Like the Crawley sisters on *Downton Abbey*. You know how they always talked about how bored they were because they had nothing to do? I think that's how I'd be if I didn't work and lived off of a trust fund."

"But the Crawley sisters all worked later on in the series. Sybil was a nurse during World War I and then was some kind of Irish Republican activist with her chauffeur husband. Edith had that job as a publisher, and Mary managed the estate." If there was one thing Samantha knew about, it was *Downton Abbey*. She'd seen the entire series from start to finish three times, and owned the movie and had seen that five times. She even owned the companion book. The Earl of Grantham was her ideal – wealthy, handsome, and very kind. He was a bit too old for her, so she'd like to find a younger version of him. Maybe somebody who was more like Matthew, Mary's doomed husband. He was young and handsome and also very kind.

"Exactly. The girls started working in season three, I

guess, because they were so bored they had to have something to amuse them. Everybody needs something to make themselves feel they're worthwhile. I don't know, Samantha. I'd be suspicious of anybody who just lived off a trust fund."

"But it's perfect. I mean, if he were working for a living, that's all he would be doing. Working. No, I'd much rather have a guy who has time for me."

Del raised an eyebrow. "Well, cute little Samantha, I wish you all the luck in the world. You deserve a great love. Like I have with Joe, who works all the time, saving lives. I mean, I hardly ever see him, but when I do, we have a really good time together. There's something to be said for not being around somebody all the time. You know what I mean?"

Samantha detected a note of cynicism coming from Del. She didn't want anybody to rain on her parade. "Well, I'm excited. But why do you think that Grayson hooked up?"

Del cocked his head at Samantha. "You know he has a Tinder account, don't you? Isn't that what a Tinder is for? To find somebody to hook up with on a moment's notice?"

Samantha furrowed her brow. She didn't like hearing that maybe Grayson was on a date. And then she immediately felt selfish for begrudging him having a life. Wasn't she always trying to encourage him to go out and make some friends? Didn't she always prod him to get out of that room and live a little? He had his job at the bookstore, but that was the only time he left the house on a regular basis. This beautiful little island offered so much, and she was always concerned he was just not taking advantage of any of it. He didn't go down to the beach that much, he didn't walk around and admire all the historical homes, he didn't really go to restaurants or bars or even go shopping. He just worked at the bookstore and then wrote his fantasy novel.

So she was happy he was getting out finally.

But, at the same time, she didn't know how she felt about him going out with a woman.

"Yes. That is what Tinder is for," Samantha said. "Well, good for him."

Del raised an eyebrow. "Is it? Good for him?"

"Of course. He's my best friend, and I want him to be happy. And he wants the same for me." Samantha raised her shoulders and grimaced. All at once, she thought about the reality that if she ended up with Adrian, and Grayson found somebody, too, she'd probably grow apart from her dearest friend. And that thought made her sad.

She thought about her Friday night ritual with Grayson back in Brooklyn. Even though she was working two jobs and delivering food through Uber Eats, she made sure Friday nights were free. She told both of her jobs she couldn't work on Friday evenings. And Grayson did the same – he was working at a bookstore in New York, too.

And the reason why both she and Grayson refused to work on Friday evenings was because that was their evening. They would sit down in front of the television and binge on a Netflix series together. They would pop some popcorn, open up a bottle of wine, and order a pizza. And then they would watch a series from 5 o'clock in the evening to 11 o'clock at night, or whenever both of them got tired. They would watch a different series every week - Samantha would choose one week, Grayson the next. Samantha would usually choose something light or female-centric, such as *Emily In Paris, Bridgerton* or *Outlander*. Grayson would choose something sci-fi or fantasy. *Lucifer, Merlin, Stranger Things* and *The Last Kingdom* were some of his chosen series.

Samantha found that Grayson's choices expanded her tastes. She never knew she liked fantasy and sci-fi until she gave Grayson's shows a chance. Grayson didn't know he liked chick shows until he watched the shows Sam picked out. Samantha liked to think they were good for each other that way.

Well, they were good for each other in a lot of other ways too.

Just then, she heard Joe coming in the door. That was her cue to leave, because she knew Del often stayed up just until Joe got home from working at the hospital where he was an ER doc, and then they both went to bed.

Samantha took a deep breath. "Well, thanks for the info. I guess I'll probably head back to my little house, and I'll be seeing you later."

"Well, don't be a stranger, pretty little Samantha. You can drop in on me anytime you want. The door's always open."

Grayson still wasn't home when Samantha finally fell asleep at three in the morning.

And she didn't know how she felt about that.

CHAPTER 17

SAMANTHA

Grayson didn't get home until 7 o'clock in the morning. Samantha heard him tiptoe in, and she came out to the living room to catch him before he went into his bedroom.

"Hey," she said in the lightest tone possible. "How was your night?"

Grayson just smiled, but Samantha caught a whiff of girl's perfume on his clothes. For some odd reason, the smell of that perfume on his jacket filled Samantha with dread.

"I asked you a question," Samantha said teasingly.

"I met somebody at the bookstore. We went to the beach after the store closed and back to her place. And I crashed on her couch. That's all that happened. It was cool. She was fun to talk to."

Samantha just nodded her head. Somehow, the elation she felt over going on a date with Adrian was muted. "Are you going to see her again?"

"I doubt it. She's only in town for the weekend, visiting some friends. Anyhow, I'm very tired. And today's my day off, so I'm not going to do anything but sleep and maybe read a book later on. I'm not going to even work on my novel."

Samantha watched him go into the bedroom. She didn't tell him about going out with Adrian at night. It was funny. She was so excited about going out with Adrian yesterday. But today, she wasn't sure how she felt about it.

*****

Around 6 o'clock, Samantha started to get ready for her date. She pulled on a pink and blue Lilly Pulitzer shift dress, matching pink pumps, and her trusty pearls. The strand of saltwater pearls, which she picked up during a trip to Mexico for $45, was her go-to accessory. She rarely left the house without them.

"These are your lucky pearls," she said to her reflection in the mirror. "They're going to snag you a billionaire. Or, at least, the son of a billionaire, which is just as good."

She walked out into the living room and saw Grayson on the couch. He looked at her and smiled. "Hot date with a rich dude?" he asked. "You look cute."

Samantha nodded her head. "Adrian Ripley. From the other night - the guy who saved my life."

"Ah. Well, have a good time."

" I will. And what are you doing tonight?"

"You're looking at it," he said. "My hot date is with this book. It's a good one, too. You need to read it after I get done. I think you'll love it - it's right up your alley."

Samantha sat down next to him. "*The Seven Husbands of Evelyn Hugo*. What's it about?"

"Old Hollywood glamour, a scandalous relationship and drama galore. I won't give too much away, but it's a good one."

"Is it about her seven husbands?" Samantha asked.

"You'll see when you read it," he teased. "I can't give away the plot so easily. But, trust me, you'll love it."

THE BEACHSIDE REUNION..

Samantha nodded. If Grayson said she'd love it, then she'd love it. He knew her so well that he always knew what recommendations to make for books, movies and television shows.

"Okay, well, I'll be shoving off for my date."

Grayson's eyebrows wrinkled. "What do you mean, shoving off? He's not coming to pick you up?"

"No," Samantha said. "We're going to meet at the restaurant."

Grayson raised one of his eyebrows and then went back to his book. "Well, have fun," he said, without looking at Samantha.

Samantha immediately felt defensive by Grayson's reaction. She could tell he didn't approve of her date with Adrian, to say the least. "What?" she asked.

Grayson put down his book. "He just doesn't sound like..." Then he cocked his head. "Do you remember that *Sex and the City* episode where Miranda was going out with a guy who didn't want to come up to her apartment and Carrie's boyfriend told her he wasn't that into her?"

Of course, Samantha remembered that episode. She and Grayson watched that show together on quite a few evenings. She had to watch hours of the BBC's *Sherlock* in exchange for their *SATC* nights, but that was a small price to pay. Besides, she loved *Sherlock,* too - she was a big Benedict Cumberbatch fan. She also had to watch Bruce Lee movies in exchange for the *SATC* nights, and she was surprised how much she enjoyed those Kung Fu movies. Bruce Lee really was a charismatic guy, and it was a shame he died so young.

"Yeah," Samantha said. "If I can recall, that stupid phrase powered an entire movie and book. Relationships aren't that simple, by the way."

Grayson went back to his book. "Well, I think the phrase is appropriate here."

Samantha was infuriated. Grayson knew just how to push her buttons, and one of the ways to do that was to be dismissive. He knew just what he was doing at this point.

She looked at her watch. "I don't have time to argue about this right now," she said. "I have to meet Adrian."

Grayson kept reading his book and said nothing.

Samantha left for her date, feeling angry with Grayson for being such a tool. What did he know about Adrian? Nothing, that's what. He'd never met him. He didn't know Adrian from Adam.

While she drove along, she tried to calm the nagging voice that was telling her one thing.

Grayson was right.

CHAPTER 18

SAMANTHA

Samantha arrived at Lola 41 a little before 7. Like practically every other restaurant in the historic district, the restaurant structure looked more like a large house than a building. Lola's was housed in a wood-shingled structure with two bay windows and a regular door. Only the sign out front signaled that this was a restaurant and not a residence.

But, inside, it was beautiful. Hardwood floors, white tablecloths, and a large bar were inside. The place was packed, as it was a Saturday night.

Samantha looked around and didn't see Adrian anywhere. She felt nervous, so she sat down at the bar and ordered a glass of white wine while she waited for her handsome prince. She looked at her watch and checked her cell phone to see if there were any messages from Adrian. There weren't.

She shrugged while she drank her wine. She was slightly early and had high hopes he would be as well. However, she was getting the impression that maybe punctuality was not this guy's strong suit.

By 7:30, she was still sitting there at the bar, still checking her watch and her phone. He was now a half-hour late and still did not text her to explain why he was running late. She decided to go ahead and call him, which she did, but she only got his voicemail. And then she texted him. "Hey, I'm here at Lola's. I hope I got the time and restaurant right. Hopefully, I'll see you soon!"

Grayson's words about Adrian not being that into her were ringing in her ears. So were her mother's words, as her mom always told her she needed to stand up for herself more. She just let men walk all over her, all the time. If the guy did show up without a good explanation or an apology, she should let him have it. But she knew she wouldn't. She knew she would just pretend nothing happened because she didn't want to rock the boat.

She also heard other pieces of her mother's advice over the years. Her mother was always telling her that when she found the right guy, she wouldn't have to lecture him all the time because he wouldn't give her reason to. Yes, she would have fights with the right guy, but he would respect her enough that the fights would be minimal.

And her mother always told her that one of the most disrespectful acts was lateness. Especially when said lateness was not accompanied by a phone call or text.

Around 7:45, Adrian finally arrived at the restaurant. "Hey," he said. "Did you put our name in?"

That was it. No apology. No explanation. No breathless words about how he had to take his grandmother to the hospital and he didn't have access to a cell phone because it died, or any excuse like that. No. None of that.

Samantha cleared her throat. And then she plastered on a smile. "I'm sorry, I didn't even think about it."

Adrian rolled his eyes. "Really? I was hoping I'd be sitting down by now."

Oh, there it was. That was the reason he was 45 minutes late. He figured she would get there, put her name in, and he could just waltz on in, 45 minutes late, just in time to get a seat without having to wait. Samantha realized that, and she bit her tongue. She plastered on a smile again.

"I wanted to wait until you got here for us to put our name in," Samantha said.

Adrian just shook his head. "Okay," he said between gritted teeth. "I guess I'll just have to do it. Excuse me."

At that, Adrian stalked away from her and towards the hostess. He came back in a matter of minutes. "It's an hour wait," he said. "Thanks a lot. Sorry, but if you would've put your name in when you got here, we'd be sitting down to eat right now."

Samantha just smiled. "And how was your day?"

He shrugged his shoulders. "Went sailing, did too much day drinking, feeling pretty hungover. Excuse me."

He then went down to the end of the bar, so he could get the bartender's attention better, and came back to the seat with a drink.

Samantha looked at her own drink, which was empty.

Adrian took a sip of his drink, and then smiled. "Nothing like a good craft whiskey," he said as he stared at his glass full of amber liquid.

Samantha looked again at her own empty drink and quietly pushed the glass away from her so the bartender would take it. She wanted another glass of wine, but she wasn't going to make a fuss about it. And the bartender was so busy, she figured it would be a while until she could get another glass of wine.

"So, sailing," Samantha said brightly. "How much fun is it? I've never been, but I've always wanted to go. There's probably nothing like being on the open water, the wind in your hair, the sun on your face, a drink in your hand."

Adrian glared at her. "You really have a romanticized version of life, don't you? Trust me, sailing is not all wind in your hair and sun on your face. It's a lot of work."

Samantha leaned forward. She was going to make the best of this evening. She was even hoping he would want to see her again. So, she mustn't make a fuss.

"I guess I don't know what all goes into sailing," she said. "Is it a hobby of yours? I mean, I'd love to know more about it. I'd like to know anything that makes you tick." She put her hand on his arm to emphasize the point.

"I'd tell you all about it, but I doubt you'd understand. Plus, it's boring talking about sailing to people who aren't into it. Lots of technical terms."

"Try me," Samantha said.

"Nah," he said. Then he just stared at her blankly. "You know what, I'm going to take a walk. I hate having to wait around for a table."

"Okay," Samantha said. "Let's go take a walk. It's really scenic around here, and I'd love to have a native tell me more about the history of this place."

He nodded his head. "No offense, but I need to take a walk by myself. You need to wait here at the restaurant for when our name comes up. And then you can call me when the table's ready."

Samantha cocked her head. "I don't understand? Aren't they going to text you when the table's ready?"

"No, they're going to text *you*. And you need to be here at the restaurant to claim the seat, to make sure they don't give our table away. They will, you know, if you don't claim it within about five or ten minutes."

At that, he left.

Samantha watched him leave and then went back to the bar.

A guy approached her. He was tall and broad, with beautiful tanned skin and light golden eyes. His straight hair was jet black.

"Adrian's really a jerk, isn't he?" the guy asked.

"I don't know what you mean?" Samantha asked.

"Oh, I think you do. You have the same look on your face that every girl who goes out with him has. Let me guess - he showed up almost an hour late and expected just to get sat right away because you were supposed to put your name in when you got here."

Samantha nodded. "Yeah. How did you know?"

"That's his way. That's how he manages to get sat right away in a crowded restaurant without a reservation – he gets a dupe to get the table for him. He's gone. I doubt he's coming back."

"Really? You think he's really gone?"

The guy shook his head. "No. But he should be. Nah, he'll be back, just because he's hungry. And you're doing all the dirty work, sitting around in this restaurant, waiting for a text."

"I don't understand. Why doesn't he just make a reservation?"

"He has no need to. He always has his date reserve the table when she gets to the restaurant. That way, he doesn't need to bother with the whole making a formal reservation thing. He's really lazy, and that's probably why he doesn't bother to make a reservation."

In spite of herself, Samantha laughed. "I guess he thought I was an easy mark."

"Guess so. By the way, my name is Marcus Tangier. But you can call me Mark."

"Samantha," she said extending her hand. "Good to meet you."

"You, too."

Samantha and Mark talked like old friends for the next

hour. He explained he was there with some friends, not a woman. For some reason, he emphasized this fact.

Samantha finally got a text saying their table was ready, and she forwarded that text to Adrian. 10 minutes later, Adrian came in the door.

"Well, Mark, it was good to meet you," Samantha said when she saw Adrian looking at her with a look of impatience on his face. "Thanks for making this rather awful night less so."

"Good to meet you, too," Mark said, handing her his business card. "And, not for nothing, but if you get tired of being a doormat, give me a call."

Samantha took a look at the business card and saw Mark was the CEO of a dot. com start-up Samantha recognized as being a Fortune 500 company.

Samantha smiled to herself as she realized that Adrian definitely was not her man.

But maybe Mark was.

CHAPTER 19

*J*essica was having a hard time focusing. She really thought she was rounding the bend with her OxyContin addiction. Being around Andrew took her mind off of that deep hole she felt in the middle of her heart, the hole she always felt. Yet, the last conversation with him had unsettled her greatly. She somehow knew his story was connected to her own. So, while she was really anxious to hear the rest of the story, she was terrified of it too.

She had joined Alcoholics Anonymous when she first arrived at Ava's home. She found this very welcoming community, and she'd gotten to know everybody's stories. When she told the group about her problems, she only explained that she had gotten addicted because of the skiing accident that caused so much physical pain for such a long period of time. She never told the group about the emotional pain she carried with her for her entire life. Mainly because she didn't really know what to say about it. She literally had no idea why she carried around that pain. Now, somehow, her friendship with Andrew was bringing her closer to it, and she felt she needed to use her AA group as a sounding board.

So, that evening, she went to a meeting as usual. She greeted her friends there, got a cup of coffee and a donut, and took her seat with the others. The meeting came to order, they held hands and said the serenity prayer, and, one by one, the people in the group told their stories. Each person explained how things were going with them that week.

Some of the people in the group were doing quite well and were happy to report they had not had any temptations to use or drink that week. Others were going through some kind of challenges in their lives, and were having a harder time trying to stay away from substances. Jessica listened to everybody talk and sometimes interjected with advice, while other times she was quick with some positive words of encouragement. She could identify with each and every person there. After all, they were all going through the same thing, in some shape or form. All of them were trying to navigate a world they were ill-equipped to get through without some kind of substance helping them along. Jessica valued their support more than she could ever express.

When it was her turn to talk, she took a deep breath. "I really have been doing great. I've been staying with Ava, like I've been telling you about. Her house is beautiful, and I'm keeping busy with doing all kinds of different jobs. The time just goes by so fast. And, as I was saying, I have a friendship with a guy. It's just a friendship, though. Still."

Shayla, one of her friends in the group, nudged her with a smile. "I'm sure you want to be more. I know we're not supposed to start anything new with anybody in the first year of sobriety, but I think that after you get your one-year chip, you're going to be hitting that one hard."

Everybody in the group laughed, including Jessica. Shayla was not one to mince words. "Actually, it's a bit more complicated than that," Jessica said after the laughter died down. "I do like him. He's a very good person. Very talented. He listens. But..."

At that, Jessica stopped talking. Everybody was looking at her expectantly. They all seemed to want to know what the hangup would be with this mysterious person that Jessica had been hanging out with.

"But, what?" Shayla asked.

"There's something about him. He went through something at a park. He didn't quite finish what he was saying because I didn't let him finish. I was terrified for him to finish. But I went through something at a park as well. Codfish Park is what's been coming to me. I know something happened there. And I could probably find out pretty easily on the Internet what did happen there, but I've been so afraid of it. I was so terrified about finding out that I just hadn't Googled it. And I'm still terrified, but I'm ready to hear about that park. I don't know if anybody here knows what might have happened there about 20 years ago?"

One of the meeting participants nodded his head. His name was Milton Parks. He was an older guy, probably in his 60s. He was clean-cut and fastidious with his dress - he usually showed up to the group with a button-down shirt with a pressed collar, pants with a crease, and shoes that showed no sign of wear. He also seemed to be a bit of a buff about the area. He was fascinated with Nantucket history. He was one of those guys who would always go on Walkabout tours around historic neighborhoods that was led by a narrator who would explain about all the historic homes, who had lived in these homes and what life was like during the earlier days.

If anybody would know about this incident, it probably

would be him. Jessica came into the meeting knowing this. Which meant that she was sure she would get her question answered. And if her question was going to be answered, she was anxious for it to be answered right there when she was amongst friends and supporters.

"Yes. Are you sure you want to hear about this?" Milton asked her.

" No. I'm not sure at all. But I think I need to."

"Okay. I'm pretty sure you're talking about the shooting at Codfish Park."

The shooting. Jessica took a deep breath. "The shooting. What happened?"

"A gunman came there. He was the father of a little boy, and apparently his wife was divorcing him. His wife told him she was going to sue for full custody because he was abusive. I guess that made him crazy because he went to that park, knowing the little boy would be at a child's birthday party. His plan apparently was to kill the little boy right in front of his mother because he wanted to punish both of them. And he wanted the mother to suffer more, which she would have if she lost her only son."

As Milton told the story, Jessica closed her eyes. Suddenly, in her mind's eye, she could see it. She was sitting at a picnic table. Then she was running around with her little friends. There were presents stacked up on a table, along with a huge cake for her. She had 10 of her little friends there, including her best friend, Andrew.

Andrew. Could it be????

His mother was talking to her mother.

"And what happened with the father?" Jessica asked, not wanting to hear the answer.

"He came in with a gun. He could not actually get to the son because another woman was there at the scene, and she stepped in front of the bullet. She was instantly killed."

And then she saw it.

Her mother was the one who stepped in front of that bullet.

CHAPTER 20

SAMANTHA

Samantha called Mark about a week after she met him. To her surprise, Adrian wanted to go out again, but Samantha turned him down. He really was a jerk. He was completely self-centered, not even asking a single question about her the entire evening. He gave her a good night kiss and slobbered all over her.

But Mark...he seemed like a sweet guy. And she could talk to him easily. So, she called him, and he asked her out on a date. And, better yet, he was willing to pick her up!

"Now, that's more like it," Grayson told her when she told him she had a date with Mark and he was going to pick her up. "When will you admit I told you so about Adrian?" he teased.

Samantha rolled her eyes but smiled. "You told me so and so did my mom. You both were right. My mom was right when she told me that if a guy doesn't work but lives off a trust fund, he's probably not a good guy to go out with. And you were right when you told me that if he didn't want to pick me up, it wasn't really a date."

Mark picked her up one Saturday afternoon for a day of

sailing. He patiently showed her all about tacking and jibing, and showed her around the boat, using the proper terms. She learned about which side was port and which side was starboard, and that the front of the boat was called the bow and the back was the aft. She found out a boom was used for adjusting the sail. She watched with fascination as he expertly tacked and jibed the boat around choppy waters.

"You'll get the hang of it, Samantha. There's a learning curve, I won't lie, but once you master it, it's pretty basic.

After the sailing adventure, they'd gone out a few more times, as he treated her to expensive dinners at five-star restaurants, and she was wowed by him.

She got filet mignon and Vermont cheddar cauliflower soup at the Ships Inn Restaurant, a restaurant in the boutique hotel called Ships Inn.

Then she had dinner with him at Topper's, a part of the Wauwinet resort on Nantucket Bay. There she got a lobster spiced with Tandoori and was served with coconut and carrots, and Diver scallops served with asparagus, potatoes, caviar and champagne. She got a Baba Rum for dessert, a coconut custard served with roasted pineapple and guava sorbet.

Samantha felt she was part of a whirlwind courtship with this guy. He was funny, charming, wealthy, and handsome. And he seemed to be really into her.

Maybe Adrian was not her prince. In fact, she knew he wasn't. But this guy seemed to be.

He finally kissed her after their fourth date, and she felt this kiss to her toes. "I really like you, Samantha," he said to her. "I'd like to see a lot more of you."

Her heart leaped out of her chest when he said that to her. She no longer had to fantasize about sailing with a rich guy, as she was doing that with him. She went to five-star restaurants with him, just like in her dreams. And, unlike Adrian, and unlike the rich guys her mother had warned her about, Mark was a very sweet guy. A real gentleman.

Even Grayson seemed to approve of him. He told Samantha that Mark seemed to be the real deal and a good catch. "Congratulations," he said. "It looks like you're finally getting your dream."

"Yes, it seems that way, doesn't it?" Samantha said. "I knew I could make it happen. I knew if I wished hard enough, I could make it happen."

And she did.

CHAPTER 21

SAMANTHA

One day, after a few weeks of romancing with Mark, Samantha arrived at her bakery job and was informed that Cynthia-the-hack was no longer working there. Javier, her boss, was beside himself.

"I have a wedding I'm making a cake for," he said in his thick Brazilian accent. "It's this weekend, and Cynthia just quit this morning. No notice. She said she got a job in Boston, and she had to leave right away."

Samantha nodded her head and stood up a bit straighter. This was her chance. She knew how to make cakes because she made all the cupcakes for the place and had been making cupcakes for 8 years. She knew how to layer the cakes and make them so that they stood up perfectly straight, because of all her binge-watching of Cake War shows and all the practice cakes she had made in her kitchen over the years. And while she'd never technically decorated a big cake, she had beautiful designs she'd drawn on paper.

She was ready, and she would make the most of this opportunity. "I'm ready, Javier. I'm your girl." She proudly pointed to her chest.

Javier just shook his head. "No. You have no experience in making wedding cakes. And Cynthia is a professional." Cynthia graduated from the Institute of Culinary Education in New York, the most prestigious school in America. She also took a four-week intensive cake-decorating course, plus a class on making fondants, using the spatula and piping techniques.

Javier's arms started to flap around. "Where am I going to find somebody on short notice? I can't just get anybody. It's a billionaire's daughter who's getting married. Oh, this is bad. This is so bad."

Samantha nodded her head. "Are you talking about the Lawrence wedding?" Charles Lawrence was one of many billionaires who summered on the island. His daughter, Ardis, was getting married at the Whaling Museum and Rooftop Deck that weekend. Every society person who was anybody was going to this shindig, from what Samantha understood.

She got very excited about the prospect of making a cake for this wedding.

"Just relax," Samantha said. "I can handle it. You have a book about what the bride likes, right?"

Javier always kept a book for every wedding, where the bride was encouraged to put pictures of things she liked and what kinds of flavors she preferred. Javier always told his clients to not put wedding cake pictures in the book, per se, but to cut out magazine pictures of things that meant something to the bride. Pictures of animals, plants, birds, butterflies, flowers and paintings often made it into this book. But also, sometimes, some pictures would tell Javier that the bride was in the mood for something different. There might be pictures of rock stars in there, or dragons or favorite movies or song lyrics or poetry. Javier encouraged the bride to be creative and access their inner child when making the book.

Samantha just needed to look at the book to get a handle on the bride, what she wanted and who she was. Javier's cakes were sought-after because they offered the element of surprise. Since Javier's policy was that the bride didn't have input on the cake, other than completing the book, how the cake looked was always a complete surprise. 100% of the time, the bride was absolutely delighted with the cake, and, since it was a surprise, it was like Christmas morning for her to see it for the first time.

This method of making a bridal cake wasn't for everyone, of course. Many, perhaps most, brides wanted to dictate everything about their cakes, from the colors to the flavors to the piping. But for the brides who liked creativity and surprise, Javier's bakery was go-to.

Javier was on the phone, though, hurriedly speaking Spanish. He was gesturing with his hands. After about a few minutes, he slammed down the phone. Then he picked it up and called somebody else, speaking English this time.

"I need a cake decorator fast," Javier said to the person over the phone. Then he shook his head and slammed down the phone again.

10 phone calls later, and he faced Samantha. "Okay. You can make the cake. But if you mess this up." He sliced his hand across his neck. "I'm hiring you for this against my better judgment. You do make beautiful cupcakes and delicious pastries, so you have the basics down."

To this, Samantha clapped her hands together. "Oh, yes, thank you, thank you, thank you. I won't let you down."

Javier looked at the ceiling as if he were praying. "Oh, what am I doing? The first big wedding of the season, everybody is going to be there, and the cake is being made by an amateur."

Samantha tried not to be insulted by his sneering referral to her as "an amateur." It was accurate. After all, she *was* an amateur. This would literally be her first wedding cake. Yet, she was confident. She'd watched enough shows to know what she was doing.

She excitedly took the book for Ardis and went into the back to study it. She was struck by how many pictures in that book harkened back to the 1920s. Ardis cut out several photos from *The Great Gatsby* movie and had also cut out pictures of art deco buildings. She'd also included pictures of silent film stars Lillian Gish, Marion Davies and Mary Pickford. Plus, she took a picture of herself in her wedding dress, and the dress had a distinctly 1920s silhouette. The bust, the length, the beading - all looked to her like a 1920s bride.

Samantha had no idea why Ardis had such a fascination with the 1920s, but it was clear that she did. She also indicated that she wanted the cake to look different from anything she'd seen in prior weddings. No pink roses, no white frosting, no piping. She wanted a stand-out, something memorable that would wow her guests. Something that would inspire her guests to take a picture and put it on social media because the cake was that special.

"So, wants non-traditional, love the 1920s era," Samantha said to herself as she reviewed the book. "Does she want color? Maybe black and gold?" But then she saw the bride loved the color purple. In another section of the book, the area that Javier labeled "color," the bride had cut out pictures of everything purple. Purple birds, purple dresses, purple jewels, purple cars. She seemed to favor the deeper purple, like the color of eggplant.

The flavor profile for the bride included deep chocolate and blood orange. She smiled as she remembered telling Adrian about her dream wedding cake that featured just these flavors.

She hummed to herself as she drew a cake that had four layers. The frosting would be a deep purple fondant made out of blood orange buttercream, and the cake would be dark chocolate with blood orange filling. She would make edible gold and silver sugar gems, which would look like diamonds, and drape them over the bottom of the cake like a flapper's beaded headdress. Then, on the second layer, she'd create edible sugar pearls that would look like a string of flapper's pearls and drape those all the way around. She'd alternate the sugar gems with the sugar pearls, and, on the top layer, she'd create an edible silver sugar brooch.

She knew how to make edible sugar pearls, sugar brooches and sugar diamonds. She knew how to make the fondant. She knew how to make the cake. She knew everything.

She'd always assumed that if she wanted to get a job making wedding cakes, she'd have to graduate from a culinary school. That made her feel hopeless because she didn't know when she could fit culinary school into her busy life. But if she did an excellent job with this cake and word got around that she was the one who created it, she predicted Javier would make her the full-time wedding cake decorator.

And, since Javier's bakery was *the* bakery that brides used on the island, and he was already booked up for the entire wedding season, her name would be on everyone's lips. It'd only be a matter of time before she could open up her own wedding cake bakery and maybe even get on one of the Food Network or Netflix cake shows she was so fond of.

Samantha took a deep breath and spent the entire day creating the cake. She couldn't believe how easy it all seemed. It was as if she was born to do this.

She was always a cake decorator. She just hadn't the chance to prove it until that moment. It was no different than somebody who was an innate piano player who finally sat down to play.

It was like a duck taking to water.

When she finally finished, she looked at the cake and knew something was missing. She could top the cake with the traditional bride and groom, but that didn't seem quite right. So, she made some edible silver sugar feathers and created a plume to top the cake.

The end result was classy yet dramatic. The deep purple color of the cake was definitely different, but all the decor she made would've been just as beautiful and elegant on a white cake. And the feathers on top definitely brought the theme together.

Javier came in to see what Samantha had created, and his eyes got wide. "How did you do this? How did you know how to make these sugar jewels and pearls and feathers?"

"I watch a lot of shows," Samantha said proudly. "I know everything there is to know about cake decorations. I've been trying to tell you that."

Javier smiled and hugged her. "It's beautiful," he said. "And if it's as delicious as it looks, the bride will be overjoyed."

"Count on it," Samantha said proudly.

CHAPTER 22

SAMANTHA

A potential crisis was blowing up at Javier's bakery. Hearing that Cynthia couldn't work on her cake, Ardis Lawrence contacted Javier. She was a sweet girl, not at all Bridezilla, but she was understandably concerned.

"Javier," Ardis said tentatively over the phone. "Uh, I don't want to cause you additional stress, but my mother wanted me to call. She heard it from the grapevine that your cake decorator left you in the lurch. I just wanted to know if there was anything I could do to help you get the cake ready."

Samantha was making some cupcakes when the phone call came in, and Javier had put Ardis on speaker so she could hear. Samantha drew a breath. Javier had loved the cake, but would Ardis? It seemed like a huge gamble.

Although the cake was beautiful, with its gleaming sugar jewels and pearls and the enormous edible diamond brooch and edible feathers, it was different from the typical bridal cake. She tried to tell herself that something different was what Ardis wanted.

Still, her stomach did flip-flops as she imagined that Ardis might hate the cake.

Then what? Her dreams would be shattered. It was almost easier before putting herself out there with this cake. She could imagine that she could set the world on fire if she just got the chance.

As long as she was never given that chance, she couldn't say she failed. But, here it was. Her chance for an absolute fail. She could no longer say she just wasn't given an opportunity.

She felt more vulnerable than ever before.

"Ms. Lawrence," Javier said. "I have it taken care of. Samantha Flynn, who's been working here for the past few months and has been working for bakeries in New York for 8 years, prepared it."

"Oh. Samantha Flynn? I've never heard of her."

That was another thing. Cynthia had a name people knew. She'd been working for Javier for the past 5 years, making all the wedding cakes for Javier's bakery. Everyone on the island knew just what they were getting with one of her cakes. Everyone knew Cynthia had graduated from a prestigious New York culinary school and had completed advanced courses in cake decorating.

"Well, uh, she's been working here, making pastries and cupcakes."

"But this is her first wedding cake?"

"Yes. I couldn't find anybody else on such short notice."

Ardis was silent for a few minutes. "The wedding is tomorrow. Oh, I wish you would've told me when Cynthia left. I probably could've found another baker to do it on short notice. Even if I couldn't have found anybody on the island on short notice, I definitely could've found a Boston baker to do it."

Of course, she could've found a Boston baker to do it. Her father owns Boston. And that wasn't a lie. The Lawrences were

THE BEACHSIDE REUNION..

old Boston Brahmin money. They came from a long line of bishops, politicians and revolutionaries, and Charles Lawrence founded a prominent hedge fund that netted him billions of dollars a year.

Javier looked green as Ardis spoke. He started to shake. "Samantha really did a lovely job," Javier weakly told her. "You'll be pleased."

"But it's her first wedding cake," Ardis said. "I know I wanted to be surprised by the cake on my wedding day, but I need to see it. There are 24 hours before the cake needs to be on the reception table, and I can find somebody in Boston to make one if they work around the clock."

Javier nodded his head. "Of course, of course. Just come by the shop, and I'll show you the cake."

"I'll be there in 15 minutes. Again, I'm so sorry for the inconvenience. My mother is the one having the cow. So, I'll be bringing her to the bakery, too. I hope you don't mind."

"Yes, yes," Javier said. "I'll see you and your mother soon."

Javier hung up the phone, put the "come back later" sign on the front door and then started talking rapidly to himself in Spanish.

Then he went into the bathroom, and Samantha could hear him retching into the toilet.

He came back out. "This could be bad, very, very bad. I should've told Ardis when Cynthia left. I should've come clean. Now what? If they hate the cake and have to go to a Boston bakery, I'm finished. One word from Ardis's mother, Catherine, and I might as well just put the 'for sale' sign on The Blue Moon Surfside. She knows everyone on the island, and she's been known to lead blackballs against people she doesn't like. I've owned this bakery and deli for 30 years, and it all could be gone just like that," he said, snapping his fingers.

Well, that was a lovely thing, Samantha thought. Where would that leave her?

Why did she insist on baking this cake? She shouldn't have been so eager to make it. If she didn't insist, Javier most likely would've called Ardis the second Cynthia left. Ardis would've found a Boston bakery and most likely wouldn't have been mad at Javier. After all, it couldn't be helped.

But now? If Ardis and her mother hated the cake, they would be pissed. Pissed because Javier's "cover-up" of the situation would've caused significant problems. Problems that nobody needed.

It was always the cover-up that gets you into trouble, Samantha thought.

Literally everything was riding on this cake.

Ten minutes later, Ardis and her mother were in the bakery. Ardis was a tall, thin strawberry blonde with narrow shoulders and long fingers. Her face looked like it was painted by an Italian master. The perfectly oval face housed big blue eyes, rose-colored butterfly lips and a delicate nose. Her strawberry hair cascaded down her back, and she was dressed in designer jeans, a silk top and a pair of shoes that would set Samantha back an entire month to buy. Taking into account all three of her jobs. Her Hermés Birkin bag would undoubtedly set Samantha back about 6 months, working all three jobs.

Her mother Catherine was dressed in a cashmere sweater set in eggplant purple and a pair of wool pants that were perfectly tailored. Like her daughter, she was thin and strawberry blonde and gorgeous. Like her daughter, her shoes and bag were out of financial reach of anybody not a millionaire. However, her hair was cut in a short bob that was perfectly styled, blown out and sleek.

Both women had perfect manicures, and each woman

wore a string of pearls – a pearl choker on Ardis and a short pearl necklace on Catherine.

Javier went over to the two women and flitted like a nervous bird. "Yes, yes," he said, handing them both a glass of champagne. "Come in, come in," he said. "And here's a sample of the cake."

Javier had Samantha make a cupcake with the flavors of the big wedding cake so that Ardis and her mother could taste it. Samantha was happy that Javier thought of it ahead of time. Maybe he knew this situation was going to happen.

Javier led the two women back to some tables, sat them down and gave them the cupcake to share. Ardis and Catherine each took a bite of the cupcake, and Ardis rolled her eyes to the ceiling.

"Oh my God," she said. "This is like a slice of heaven in a cake. What flavors are in there?"

Samantha started to wring her hands. She was feeling hopeful but still nervous. "Blood orange, dark chocolate and a hint of lavender," Samantha said. "The buttercream was made with butter, confectioner's sugar, blood orange juice and the zest of a blood orange."

"Mom, what do you think?" Ardis asked Catherine.

Catherine nodded her head. "Decadent, rich, and the flavor profile just goes together perfectly," she said. "It's like blood orange and dark chocolate were made for each other. Who knew?"

Ardis smiled. "Mom, you love those chocolate-covered orange peels. This is like those candies except in cake form."

Catherine nodded her head. "Well, Ms. Flynn, you passed the taste test. But let's see the cake."

Samantha felt a pit in her belly. It felt like somebody had taken her stomach and tied it up in knots. She took a deep breath and went back and wheeled the cake into the bakery so the women could look at it.

Ardis's mouth gaped open when she brought it out, and she put her hand up to cover it. Her blue eyes got wide, and tears started down her cheek.

What? What? She hated it, Samantha thought. Those tears were because she hated it, and she would have to find a different baker on a moment's notice. Everybody was going to be at the shop later with torches and pitchforks.

"It's beautiful!" Ardis exclaimed. "How did you make those jewels? And that brooch? And those amazing pearls? And that feather plume! How did you make all those?"

Catherine nodded her head. "The color is magnificent. Classy yet dramatic. Nobody will be able to take their eyes off it. Everyone is going to be talking about it. I can just imagine now all those women who had married off their daughters with a boring white cake. They're going to be green with envy."

Samantha beamed, and Javier hugged her tightly.

"The pearls were easy to make," Samantha said. "I just rolled some fondant in luster dust once the fondant dried. The diamonds were also easy. I used isomalt, a sugar substitute, and put it into a mold and heated it up. The brooch was a sugar paste I put into a mold and then dusted with silver luster dust. The feathers were a bit trickier, but I put some sugar paste into a feather cutter and used a sharp knife to get the details right."

"This cake goes so well with my Gatsby theme!" Ardis said. "I mean, my wedding is inspired by Gatsby. Everyone is encouraged to dress in the style of the era. My dress has an antique feel, and I'll be wearing a headband instead of a veil. We'll be leaving the party in a 1929 Rolls Royce. And my dress is cream-colored, not white. That's why I included all those 1920s pictures in my book to Javier. You really got it, Samantha. You baked the perfect cake."

Samantha felt like she was walking on air as Ardis praised her and then gave her a spontaneous hug. "Thank you," Samantha said, feeling tears spilling down her own cheeks. Was she dreaming this? Did she really ace her very first wedding cake?

Yes. Yes, she did.

Ardis looked at her mother, and her mother nodded.

"I hate to do this to you, Samantha. But the groom's cake..." She shook her head. "Not good. Boring. I know this is short notice, but I'll pay two times as much as what the other baker charged for the groom's cake if you'll make one for us. I'd love for the cake to look like a 1920's era Rolls Royce, just like the one Max and I rented for the evening. Do you think you could do that?"

Samantha knew she could. Javier had every mold known to man, and she'd watched enough shows to have the technique down. Of course, there was a short turnaround time, so she'd have to bust her butt. But she knew that she could manage it.

"Sure," she said. "What flavors?"

"Max loves raspberry," Ardis said. "And white chocolate."

Samantha smiled. "I'll get it done. I promise."

"Oh, I'd love that," Ardis said. "And you've been such a dear and a lifesaver. I'd love for you to be one of my guests at the wedding. Do you think you can make it?"

Samantha nodded eagerly, her insides doing flip-flops. "Oh, yes, I'd love that!"

She could invite Mark. That would really impress him, Samantha thought. She felt inferior to him because he had a ton of money, and she was broke. But if she took him to a billionaire daughter's wedding, this could really make him take notice.

"Well, we better get going," Ardis said. "So you can get to

work. I'm sorry to be doing this to you, but I have a feeling you got this."

"I do."

As Ardis and Catherine left, Samantha thought she'd died and gone to heaven.

And she also thought that she was finally on her way.

CHAPTER 23

SAMANTHA

Samantha had to call into her restaurant job after Ardis gave her the groom's cake job. It was super short notice, and Samantha started to panic. She knew she could do a great job on the cake, but being so pressed for time made her feel nauseated.

So, she did the first thing that came to her head. She called Grayson in to help her. Javier was manning the bakery and deli, selling the patrons the usual sandwiches, éclairs, cupcakes, Danishes, macaroons, cinnamon rolls and cookies, while Samantha toiled in the back.

"How are you doing?" Javier asked.

"Stressed," Samantha said. "I need some help. Can I call my best friend to come in here? He can help me get the ingredients together and whatever else I might need."

She knew Grayson would be able to help her because she'd made practice cakes at their home. Grayson was always good about being her taste guinea pig and was a whiz at getting all the ingredients for her. Plus, she needed him. She needed his moral support, she needed to bounce ideas off of him, and she needed to have somebody to celebrate with. He also calmed her down when she was stressed.

And right at that moment, stressed wasn't the word for how Samantha was feeling. Panicked would be a better word. She needed Grayson to ground her.

"Oh, yes, yes," Javier said, clapping his hands. "If Grayson can help you, then I'm all for it. I won't be able to pay him, of course, but if you're okay with that, and he is too, then go ahead and call him."

"Thanks," Samantha said.

Grayson was there in ten minutes. Samantha was bouncing off the walls. "Thanks for coming," Samantha said. Then she told him all about Ardis and her mother loving her cake.

"Awesome," Grayson exclaimed, giving his best friend a hug. "What are you going to wear to the wedding?"

"I don't know yet," Samantha said. "I'm going to invite Mark as my date. I hope he doesn't already have plans. Oh, I need to call him to ask him. Hold on."

Samantha saw Grayson's eyes cloud over when she mentioned taking Mark. She suddenly felt terrible she wasn't going to take Grayson, but she knew he never felt comfortable at society affairs. That wasn't his jam. Plus, if she was going to try to drum up more business for the bakery, it would help if she had a billionaire on her arm. Mark would be able to introduce her to all the right people.

Samantha called him, got his voice mail, and left a message. "Hey, Mark, this is Sam. Guess what? I got invited to the Lawrence wedding. I'd love for you to be my plus one. Give me a call."

At that, Samantha hung up the phone and went back to talking to Grayson. "Okay. Now, where were we? Oh, yes, I need some help getting this puppy together. The groom's cake. Javier has this amazing mold of a 1920s-era Rolls

Royce. Now, all I need for you to do is help me get all the ingredients together and maybe make some stiff peaks out of some egg whites. You know how to do all that. Here, let me get you an apron."

She got him an apron and noticed he was suddenly quiet. She cocked her head at him as he reluctantly put the apron on.

"Hey," Samantha said to him. "You okay?"

"Sure, sure," he said. "But you know, I'd love to go to this wedding with you."

"Oh. I'm so sorry." Samantha hung her head. Was she being completely insensitive? Yes, yes, she was. "I just didn't think you liked being around rich people. Or go to weddings. And Mark's from that world. He'll be able to hook me up with people there who I can pimp our bakery to. If you went with me, we'd just stand in a corner and make fun of everyone and crack each other up and act like fools together. This will be a business event for me, and I need to take it seriously."

She was making excuses, she knew. She really wanted a chance to impress Mark, and she thought this would be the perfect way to do it. Have him go as her date and see her in his world, and maybe he could imagine her being in his world permanently. That's how it would happen in the movies, she thought.

And if it could work in the movies, it could work in real life.

Right?

"I understand," Grayson said, but Samantha felt terrible. She felt the energy between them dissipate. He was no longer exuberantly sharing in her good fortune. He was quiet, and he looked sad.

"Oh, Grayson," Samantha said, putting her arm around him. "Listen, I'm sure I'll be invited to more of these. I hope my name will be on everyone's lips after this. I'll invite you to the next one, I promise."

"Sure," Grayson said. Then he put on his apron. "Now, where are those egg whites?"

Samantha smiled and handed him a dozen eggs.

The two of them worked together to make the cake. Grayson helped her measure out the ingredients, he beat the egg whites into a fine peak, and he helped her get the frosting together. While the cake baked, they played a few hands of Hearts.

Grayson seemed back to normal, but he still looked sad. Samantha could always sense his moods, even when he tried to hide them. And she didn't really know what to say to make it better.

So, she did her usual babbling about everything under the sun while the cake baked and then cooled. She did that when she was nervous, as she was at the moment.

But why was Grayson making her nervous?

The cake turned out perfectly, a rich white chocolate cake with a soft raspberry center. Samantha made the white chocolate raspberry buttercream frosting and spread it all over the cake. Then she used the airbrush gun to color the car, the wheels, the grill and the car top. The car's body was colored cream, the top was black, as were the tires, but she also made the tires white-wall. The grill was colored silver, as were the headlights. Also silver was the little Rolls Royce hood ornament called *The Spirit of Ecstasy.* This was the figure of a woman leaning forward with her arms behind her and her clothing billowing like a pair of wings.

By the time the cake was ready, it was 2 in the morning, and Samantha was exhausted. Grayson also seemed pretty tired, but he was still there with her, even though he could've gone home long ago.

"We did it," Samantha said, admiring her work. The

airbrush paint was perfectly applied, and the car looked like a model car, not a cake. It was a classic Rolls Royce, with spoked wheels, an elongated chassis, a prominent silver grill with a hood ornament, the spare tire on the side and a hardtop.

Grayson grinned. It was his first genuine smile in hours. "You're very talented, kid," he said, hugging her. "I predict you'll get hot after these two cakes."

Samantha hugged him back. It was then that she realized that she'd never heard back from Mark.

She shook her head. Well, it *was* on short notice. She was tempted to go ahead and invite Grayson after all, but she wanted to keep her options open in case Mark called her at the last minute.

Yes, she was *that* girl.

CHAPTER 24

SAMANTHA

Samantha was *so* excited about her first society wedding that she felt like she could burst. Javier gave her a $2,500 pre-paid debit card bonus for making the cakes. Samantha would spend it on a beautiful dress, shoes, a professional hairdresser and a makeover. She also gave Grayson $500 of the money, over his protests. After all, he helped her immensely in getting the groom cake together.

Her mother would undoubtedly scold her for spending this money and would tell her she was foolish. Maybe she was. She didn't know. She only knew she had to wow the people at the Lawrence wedding.

She couldn't wow them with the clothes and shoes she currently owned.

Samantha thought she'd go to the historic district the morning of the wedding, intent on hitting up the upscale shops that lined the cobblestone streets. However, on a whim, she decided to instead go to Boston to try to find something.

The reception started at 7 that evening, so Samantha had time. And she'd always fantasized about having the money to

THE BEACHSIDE REUNION..

go shopping in Boston. She was going to have to pay out the nose for all the Ubers she would have to take, not to mention the round-trip plane ride, which was $400, but no matter. When she was determined to do something, she did it. And she was determined that she was going to hit the Gucci, Salvatore Ferragamo and Nieman Marcus stores in Boston.

At 6 that morning, Samantha set out on her adventure. She wanted to take Grayson, but he was sulking in his room for some reason, and he curtly informed her he was writing that day and couldn't be bothered.

"Moody boy," Samantha said to herself as she called herself an Uber. No matter. Grayson's grey mood wasn't going to bring her down.

Three and a half hours later, Samantha arrived at Copley Place, an enormous indoor upscale mall in the Back Bay neighborhood of Boston. She'd flown in on the first flight in the morning, then took an Uber over to the mall. Copley Place was connected to several other large office buildings, hotels and another mall through sky bridges and other indoor tunnels.

It was also the shopping center where all the prominent fashion designers opened their stores.

She arrived at the gleaming mall, imagining herself buying shoes and bags like she saw on Ardis Lawrence and her mother, but was dismayed when she saw the price tags on the Hermés bags and Louboutin shoes at the Nieman Marcus store. She could buy a pair of Louboutins with the money her boss gave her, but they were $800. As for the Hermés bag, forget that. With a price tag of $14,000 and up, Samantha knew she could buy a car for the same amount of money. It wouldn't be a Range Rover, like what Adrian and Mark drove, but she could definitely purchase a cute previously-owned Mini Cooper.

She was further discouraged to see how much designer

dresses cost. She found a fabulous off-the-shoulder white Givenchy dress, but it cost $3,000. She went over to the Brunello Cucinelli store and found a sexy silk cowl-neck halter gown, also in white, with a $2500 price tag.

But, then again, these dresses were in white. Only the bride was supposed to wear white to a wedding. At least, that was the rule Samantha remembered. She looked it up on her phone and saw that, sure enough, it was gauche to wear white to a wedding and knew that even if she could afford these dresses, they wouldn't be appropriate.

Not that she could afford them.

She felt tears coming to her eyes. She definitely couldn't dress like one of them. Not with a mere $1,500, which was what she had left after she gave Grayson his money and she had paid for her plane ticket. And if she couldn't afford designer dresses, shoes and bags, how would she ever fit in? If she showed up in something cheap from Macy's, everybody would be secretly talking behind her back. She'd stick out like a sore thumb.

So, she decided she could try to fake it by buying a pair of designer shoes. She'd fantasized about owning a pair of Manolo Blahniks ever since her mother turned her onto *Sex and the City*. She owned every DVD for that series and watched them all the time. Maybe she could get by with a pair of Manolos, which would set her back $800, and try to find a dress for around $300.

She ended up buying a pair of navy patent-leather Mary Jane Manolos for $800 and a gorgeous navy off-the-shoulder Ralph Lauren dress for a steal at $190. The crepe dress was fitted and floor-length, with a subtle sash at the waist. The skirt had a slit, so it would be easy to walk in and made it sexy to boot.

Then, remembering the Gatsby theme, she bought a

flapper headband at a thrift store, along with a long strand of fake pearls.

After getting a professional manicure in shell pink, and a haircut, she was tapped out. She barely had the money to get back. Still, she had the pair of shoes she'd always dreamed of owning. Yes, they were frivolous, as that $800 really should've been spent on rent and food.

But a girl had to live a little once in a while.

As for the bag she was going to carry - she had an old Coach clutch at home. She'd picked it up at a thrift store, and it was in decent shape. She was going to carry that to the wedding. As much as she wanted to be able to take an Hermés or Fendi clutch like everybody else was going to have, she just couldn't afford it.

By the time she got back, she barely had the time to shower and change. Grayson was in his room, writing his novel, but he took the time to evaluate Samantha before she went out the door.

He nodded his head after she dressed and got ready. He put his hands on her shoulders as he looked at her, and, for some odd reason, Samantha felt a tingle as he stood there looking into her eyes. Perhaps for the first time, she noticed the specks of grey and hazel that danced around in his green eyes. And his smell - he was wearing some kind of cologne that was smoky and smelled vaguely of cedarwood and sage. His hands were strong, and she noticed the outline of his muscular chest hidden beneath his tight t-shirt.

He winked at her, and the spell was broken. "You look good, kid, but you could do with less lipstick. Or maybe a different color. That red doesn't quite work."

Samantha nodded and then went back into the bathroom and saw he was right. The red lipstick made her face look paler. She took some tissue and wiped it off and swiped on one in a coral color. Then she went back out.

"Better," Grayson said. "You knock them dead. When is Mark coming to get you?"

"I never heard back," Samantha said. "But I'm not surprised. It was really short notice."

"Oh. Well, I'm sure you'll have fun. Everybody's going to notice your shoes. Those look like some hella expensive pumps."

Samantha grinned. Grayson was a boy who noticed a girl's shoes. Oh, God, was he secretly gay?

"They are."

Then she remembered that she forced Grayson to watch a *Sex and the City* marathon with her on a long weekend when they had nothing else to do. In return, she had to watch everything in the Bruce Lee oeuvre. To her surprise, she really enjoyed the Bruce Lee movies and he really got into *Sex and the City*. While they watched the shows, Samantha had pointed out the girls' shoes.

Since that time, the two best friends watched *Sex and the City* together from time to time, in exchange for *Sherlock* marathons, featuring one of her favorite actors, Benedict Cumberbatch.

So that was how he recognized quality pumps.

She felt a sense of relief that he probably wasn't secretly gay, just observant, and then wondered why she felt that sense of relief.

Why did she care if he was gay or not?

She shook her head and then got into her car and drove to the reception.

Her hands were shaking on the steering wheel as she drove. What were those feelings that washed through her back there as Grayson looked into her eyes? Why did she suddenly feel the need to have his pillowy lips on her own?

Stop it. It's Grayson, for the love of God. He's like your brother.

Except he wasn't.
And that confused the hell out of Samantha.

CHAPTER 25

SAMANTHA

Samantha got to the party, and it was in full swing. There were hundreds of people milling about, and, for once, she wasn't working this party. She was a guest. A guest at a billionaire's party.

She glanced across the room, and she saw Mark. He apparently was a friend of the bride, or the groom. She wasn't sure which. But she got very excited when she saw him. He smiled at her, and made his way over.

"Samantha!" he said, coming over to her and giving her a big hug. "What are you doing here?"

"Ardis invited me. I made the cakes." And then she pointed over to the cakes.

Mark took a look at the cakes, and then looked over at Samantha with astonishment on his face. "You made those? I had no idea you were such an artist! Everybody's over there, looking at the cakes, wondering who designed them. Everybody just assumed it was some top cake designer. They're gorgeous, and I mean gorgeous. You're very talented."

Samantha could feel herself blushing.

At that, Ardis and Max, the newlyweds, entered the hall

to the applause of everybody. They danced their first dance to Fanny Brice singing *My Man*, one of the biggest hits of the 1920s. And then everybody joined them on the dance floor.

Two hours later, after Mark had introduced Samantha to everybody he knew, who was everybody in the hall, it seemed, Ardis came over to her. "Samantha, I'd like you to meet somebody. This is Gordon Ramsay. He was raving about the cakes, and he wanted to meet the artist behind it."

Samantha put her hand to her mouth, and, with a shaking hand, she shook his hand. "Mr. Ramsay, I, I, I…"

He smiled at her, and in a gentle voice, he said "you have some real talent, Samantha. You have a future in this. Ardis tells me these were your first cakes? Astounding!"

She felt her voice shaking. "Yes, they're my first cakes. But it's been eight years in the making. I mean I've been making cupcakes for eight years, and I've been designing cakes on paper for longer than that even. I never thought I'd get a chance to actually make a cake, and this whole experience has been so surreal. And meeting you, that's the icing on the cake, I mean, that was stupid for me to say. It was the gravy on my mashed potatoes."

Gordon Ramsay just laughed. "It was very inventive for you to go in that direction with these cakes. You show real flair, artistry, and creativity. The flavor profiles you chose are divine. You have a future. You had a dream. Now it's becoming a reality. And good for you. Well done you!"

After that, anything that would've happened would've put Samantha on cloud nine. But she had several other chefs come up to her, who weren't famous, but were Michelin chefs, telling her how great the cakes were.

And her evening with topped off by a walk along the beach with Mark. "Samantha, I've really enjoyed getting to know you. You're so pretty, and sweet, and talented. How come I never knew you were so talented?"

Samantha shook her head. "Nobody's known this. Nobody but-"

Then she drew a breath. She was going to tell him that nobody knew about her hidden talent but Grayson, and, all at once, she felt a pain in her heart. Grayson knew everything about her, and he always was there for her. He was the only one she was ever brave enough to share her dreams with, because she knew he wouldn't laugh at her when she told him about her goals. She always thought everybody else would have just dismissed her ideas about being a cake decorator, because the world saw her as being nothing but a flighty, silly girl. But Grayson knew better. He always knew the real her.

Now, everybody else did too.

"Nobody but who?" Mark asked.

"Nobody knew. I always kept it to myself."

Mark nodded his head and leaned down to kiss her. "You know, Samantha, I've been looking for a girl like you. Sweet, unpretentious, guileless. I could really fall in love with you."

And Samantha looked in his eyes, she knew one thing.

And she had to tell Grayson about it right away.

*****

When Samantha arrived back home after the wedding reception, she knew she had to talk to Grayson. It was 2 in the morning, and he was sleeping, but Samantha crept into his room and lay down on the bed next to him.

"Hey," Samantha said, startling him awake. "I need to talk to you."

His eyes got wide, and he rubbed them. "What time is it?"

"It's 2. You're usually awake at this time." Which was true, as Grayson tended to be a night owl. "My luck, tonight is when you decided to go to bed early."

"Well, I got my writing done early, and I was tired, so I turned in at 10. Did you have fun?"

Samantha drew a breath. "Not really. Mark was there, actually. He wasn't with a date. We spent the reception together, and he introduced me to a lot of people. He said he didn't get my text messages."

"Did everyone love the cakes?"

"Oh my God, the cakes were huge hits. I had so many people come up to me and rave about them after Ardis told her guests I was the one who baked them. Javier's bakery is going to be busier than ever after tonight, judging by the reaction to my cakes."

Grayson smiled. "I knew you would wow them."

"Yes. Gordon Ramsey was at the wedding. He was one of the ones who came up to congratulate me and tell me how much he loved my cakes. He said they showed flair, artistry and creativity, and they were delicious."

Grayson cocked his head. "*The* Gordon Ramsey?"

"*The* Gordon Ramsey," Samantha confirmed. "He's a really nice guy, by the way. Anyhow, it.was.surreal. There were also a lot of other Michelin chefs there from big restaurants, and they also complimented my cakes. So, I guess I was definitely on the right track with them."

"Hell yeah," Grayson said. "You did it, kid. You're on your way to your dream."

"I guess my obsession with Food Network cake shows paid off after all," Samantha said. Then she drew another breath. "But I really didn't have a good time."

"Huh? Come again? You just told me that Gordon Ramsey loved your cakes and that Mark hung out with you all night and introduced you around. Sounds like a next-level event in my book."

Samantha bit her bottom lip. "I didn't have a good time because you weren't there with me." She looked into his eyes, fearing rejection. What was she doing? If he didn't feel romantically towards her too, then that would ruin everything.

Or, maybe not. The two best friends could just carry on as if Samantha never said a word to Grayson about how she felt about him.

Grayson smiled. "Yeah, well, you were right. If I had been there, we would've just stood in the corner making fun of everyone and goofing around. Gordon Ramsey would've been scared off of talking to you if I was there and you were acting a fool. So, it was probably all for the best."

Samantha shook her head. "No. You don't understand." She took another big breath in. "I realized something. I don't quite know how it happened, but I think I'm in love with you."

She said the words quickly, before she could stop herself.

Grayson's mouth gaped open a little. "When did you come to that realization?"

"Tonight. I mean, I saw Mark there, but I couldn't stop thinking about you. He's really sweet and very much a gentleman. He seems to think the world of me. But, he's not you."

Grayson stared at her. "Sam, I-"

She cut him off, not wanting to hear his inevitable rejection. "I realized I loved you when all the people came up to me to rave about the cakes, and all I could think about was I wanted you by my side to share in all of it. I knew you would be just as excited as me. And when Gordon Ramsey congratulated me, all I wanted to do was spaz out about it with you."

Grayson looked at Samantha for a moment. "Is this real? Are you really telling me you love me?"

Samantha nodded and said nothing. She was terrified of his response and was prepared to tell him just to forget she said anything.

But Grayson put his hands in her hair and kissed her

softly. She sighed. She felt that kiss through every cell of her body, and her breath halted for a moment.

She closed her eyes after the kiss and murmured, "you literally took my breath away."

"You've always taken away mine," Grayson admitted.

And, just like that, Grayson and Samantha went from best friends to lovers.

It took six years for Samantha to finally realize that Grayson was The One.

It took Grayson six seconds, as he later on admitted to Samantha. It was after they made love for the fourth time that afternoon.

"You're kidding!" Samantha said, punching his hard chest with her fist. "You've been in love with me all along? Why didn't you tell me?"

Grayson just laughed. "I didn't want to ruin things, and I never thought you'd feel the same way."

Samantha shook her head. "Haven't you seen *any* movies or TV shows? The woman's always clueless about the guy's feelings, but once somebody tells her, she always realizes she loves the guy, too. That happened with Ross and Rachel on *Friends* and Niles and Daphne on *Frasier*. And just about every romantic comedy ever."

Grayson stroked Samantha's hair and stared lovingly at her. "Life isn't a romantic comedy," he said.

"No. But it's pretty damned good."

And they made love again.

CHAPTER 26

JESSICA

Ever since Jessica found out the secret of how her mother died, she couldn't bring herself to face Andrew. It was irrational, she knew. But she couldn't help but think that Andrew was the cause of her mother's death. If he wasn't at the party, her mother would still be alive right now. Her brain knew it wasn't his fault. In fact, he had been suffering for it as well. That was clear by the poems he wrote about the incident. He was not at fault. There was only one person who was at fault, and that was his father, George.

Once all the memories came tumbling out of her brain, Jessica became obsessed about finding out all the information about what happened. It wasn't hard to find out, at all. All she had to do was Google it, and she was able to find many articles about it. Andrew's father was named George Kraków. He was suffering from PTSD after serving in the first Gulf War. Apparently, that was why he was getting divorced from Andrew's mother, Vivian. George was killed by the police who came on the scene, and he was tackled from behind by a bystander before he could hurt anybody else besides her mother.

THE BEACHSIDE REUNION..

While Jessica should've been happy that nobody else was hurt in this incident, somehow, she wasn't. It just didn't seem fair. Why was her mother the only one who had to pay the price for this guy's mental illness? Why couldn't somebody have seen what he was going to do and stopped him before he ever came into the place? Why did Andrew's mother have to marry such a violent guy?

And she was finally able to figure out where she'd seen that painting before, the one with the people in the wooden shoes at the beach. Once her memories came back, they all came back. She remembered that after her mother was killed right in front of her, her father took her to a therapist. Her therapist had that exact same painting on her wall.

While she was happy her trauma was finally unearthed because she knew that it had to be, sooner or later, if she was ever to move on with her life, she also felt like she was re-traumatized. Like a rape victim on a courtroom stand who becomes re-victimized by opposing counsel's questions, she felt that her remembering this incident was like it was happening to her all over again.

And, once the memories came flooding back, there was just no stopping any of it. She could still smell the birthday cake, could see it in her mind's eye exactly as it was. The big Disney film of that year was the Hunchback of Notre Dame, so her birthday cake had a picture of Esmeralda, the beautiful Gypsy in that story. The biggest toy of that year was Tickle Me Elmo, and it was so coveted that it was hard to find in the stores, but her mother seemed to be able to find it anyhow. That was her big gift for that year, and it seemed she was the envy of her little friends. She was obsessed with the Lion King, as most kids were in the 1990s, so she also received a stuffed Simba animal. And she could see all the other presents that her friends gave her as well, from a Cabbage Patch doll to several Barbies, as well as a few Kens to go with the Barbies. She could still see herself playing on the playground equipment and running around with the other kids, sliding down the slide, blowing out the candles, just feeling like it was the best birthday ever.

She could see all of that. And she could also see her mother seeing the gun man come in, and instinctively throw herself in front of the little boy, who Jessica now knew was Andrew. She knew that for a fact because when she started to research the incident, she found several articles that referenced Andrew and his musical career. In fact, once Andrew made it big, she found entire articles that centered around him and how his almost losing his life at the age of five colored his outlook and informed his music.

What was difficult was that Andrew was living in the same house as her, and the two of them were becoming close friends before Jessica remembered all of this. And now, she just couldn't look at him. When she looked in his beautiful blue eyes, all she could see was that he was responsible for her devastation. He was responsible for the fact that she grew up without a mother. It was because of him that she went dumb for two entire years. She didn't speak a word between the ages of five and seven, and her father didn't do a thing about it. It wasn't until he got remarried to Stella, and Stella, to her credit, actually tried to force her father into doing something about his mute daughter, that she actually got a therapist. The therapist was the one who helped her find her voice again.

At some point in her life, she just blocked all of it out. And her father must've been relieved that she had repressed those memories, which was why he never spoke to her about how it was she lost her mother. But, she knew a little bit about trauma, and she knew that the trauma was always there - she just couldn't access it. However, it was eating her alive from the inside. She ran from it as much as she could, not knowing exactly what she was running from, until she could run no more. And now, when she closed her eyes, all she could see was her beautiful mother giving her life so that Andrew could be saved.

Ava apparently noticed that Andrew and Jessica were no longer buddies. It wasn't difficult to know that this was the case, as Andrew went down to the beach by himself most evenings, when before, he would go down there with Jessica and play his music.

Andrew didn't understand why Jessica had suddenly grown cold and shut him out. She wouldn't talk to him, so he left her notes underneath her door. They would inquire about what he did wrong. Was she offended by any of his poems? Did she just stop liking his music? How was she doing? His notes would also plaintively say that he missed her company when he went to the beach to play. He even wrote her a long handwritten letter stating he hoped she didn't get the wrong idea. He knew she was a recovering addict, and he knew she wasn't supposed to get into any relationship for the first year. He wanted her to know that he valued her friendship and wasn't trying to romance her. Jessica read that letter, and somehow, that just made it worse. Because, in her mind, before all of this happened, she was falling hard for Andrew.

But one thing Jessica never allowed was to have her trauma affect her work. The fact that she was so hardworking actually saved her during this time, because it took her mind off of her troubles. When she was mindlessly chopping vegetables, or waiting on tables, or doing the laundry for the guests, or manning the phone or monitoring the website for reservations, or cleaning and vacuuming, she could push all of it away. So there was nothing Ava could complain about regarding her work ethic.

So, when Ava knocked on her door one evening towards

the last part of July, and told her she needed to talk to her, Jessica felt apprehensive. Surely Ava didn't want to scold her for anything.

"No, no," Ava said when Jessica asked her if she wanted to talk to her because she was unhappy with her work. "Of course not. In fact, I'd like to go ahead and offer you a raise and a bonus, because you've been invaluable to me. But I'd like to talk to you on behalf of Andrew."

Jessica couldn't look at Ava after Ava said she was there as an emissary of sorts for the one guy she didn't want to deal with anymore. She didn't want to admit to Ava why she was giving Andrew the brush-off, because she just didn't want to talk about it. Even now, when she was very clear on what had happened to her when she was five years old, she still wanted to keep her feelings and emotions about it to herself. "What about Andrew?"

"He wanted me to talk to you. He said you won't talk to him anymore, and he's very hurt by that. I had to pry it out of him, because I've noticed the two of you are no longer going down to the beach together. He looks so lost and lonely out there by himself and my heart just went out to him. So he admitted to me you've been given him the cold shoulder, and he has no idea why. You do understand that Andrew is only here for the next few weeks. After that, I guess he goes back to his home in Los Angeles. I hope you can patch things up with him before he leaves."

Jessica didn't know what to say to Ava about it. How could she tell Ava that every time she looked at Andrew, she saw her loss? How could she explain to Ava that she blamed Andrew for her mother dying, even though he had nothing to do with it and he was also a victim? Andrew didn't even know Jessica was the daughter of the woman who saved his life by giving her own. If he did know that, maybe he would understand why it was that Jessica just couldn't look at him anymore. After all, Andrew was a sensitive sort. His sensitivity was the reason why he was such a great songwriter. He had empathy and heart for people, and that came out in every word he sang.

So, when Ava made her request that Jessica make things right with Andrew before he left for good, Jessica said nothing, but just nodded her head.

"I hope that you can take my words to heart. Don't forget that we're going to be having a party here this Saturday for Quinn's birthday. It's going to be closed to the public, but of course my closest friends and family will be there. Quinn, her daughter Emerson, Hallie, her business partner and friend Willow. Andrew said he would be there as well."

When Ava said that Andrew would be at the party, her words took on a hopeful lilt.

"I'll have to think about whether or not I'm going to attend. My AA group is having a gathering that evening at a sponsor's home. No offense, but there's not going to be anybody at your party who understands what it's like to struggle with sobriety and depression when you're supposed to be joyful and giving thanks. The people in my group do understand that. They live that. So, I appreciate your invitation, but I think I'll probably join my AA group that night."

Ava nodded her head and stood up. "I do understand. But I hope you know I really do care about you. Andrew cares about you. Everybody cares about you. And if you ever need somebody to talk to, I'm always available."

Ava got up and left, and Jessica lay on her bed staring at the ceiling. She still could not get the picture of her mother dying out of her mind. Every time she closed her eyes, she saw it again, and again, and again.

And she knew that she was never going to get that vision out of her head.

CHAPTER 27

JESSICA

Jessica was feeling extremely depressed. She had nightmares every night, and in her nightmares, she could see her mother killed again and again. She would always be rushing up to her mother's dead body, her five-year-old body covering her mother's chest as she sobbed. She would always wake up wanting desperately to use. A very strong part of her wanted to just leave the house, just leave it behind, live on the streets again, if she could just be reunited with her beloved OxyContin. She desperately longed for the oblivion the drug afforded her.

However, she managed to shake off the feeling of needing the drug, and proceeded to throw herself into her daily chores. For that morning, she was supposed to start taking reservations after she finished cleaning the floors and doing laundry for the guests. While she was busy vacuuming the floor, a young girl came through the door with a violin case in her hand. She was a slight girl, very pretty in her way, black hair, blue eyes, black makeup and black clothes.

"Hey," she said to Jessica."I'm going to be playing tonight."

Jessica nodded her head, and simply pointed to the dining room, and kept on vacuuming.

The young girl just stood there, looking at Jessica quizzically. "You okay?" she asked her.

Jessica took a deep breath, in through her nose and out through her mouth. Somehow, her head was swimming completely, and she felt like biting this young girl's head off for bothering her. She opened her mouth to say something bitingly sarcastic, but then she looked into the blue eyes of the girl, saw a deep well of empathy in those eyes, and sat down on a nearby chair and just sobbed. She realized while she was crying that these were the very first tears that she'd ever cried for her mother. She didn't cry when it happened – she went mute instead. And then she buried what had happened for so long that she never did cry all these years, either.

The young girl just nodded her head. "I thought so."

"How did you know?" Jessica managed to gasp out between sobs. "How did you know?"

"I lost my parents. I found my mother in the bathroom. She had a heart attack after she found out my father had died while out for a run. There was just something about the way you looked at me just now. I could just see that something was going on with you like what happened to me. I don't know, call it a sixth sense, call it intuition, call it what you want, but I just knew you were tormented just like I am. What happened?"

Jessica just shook her head. She was sobbing uncontrollably, and she just couldn't stop. But, finally, she did stop. "My mother was killed in front of me." That was the first time she had uttered those words to anybody. Even when she was with her AA group, which was where she had found out what happened, she didn't say those words out loud to them.

Somehow, saying those words liberated her. "My mother was killed in front of me."

The young girl just placed her hand on top of Jessica's. "Dude, I'm so sorry."

"No. I'm sorry about you. How old are you, anyhow?"

"13. Yeah, it really sucked to find my mother in the bathroom like that. I was all alone, too. And you know, in that moment, I didn't know what to do. I totally forgot about 911. I just couldn't think, so I just sat there on the bathroom floor with her for hours."

"How did you get help?" Jessica asked her.

"I finally did call 911 and then I walked out of the house. I guess I was in a complete daze. I walked out into the middle of the street, and a car almost hit me. I had no idea where I even lived at that point. I had no identification on me. They had to take me to the police station, and they fingerprinted me just so that they could find out who I was. Then I sneaked out of the police station, got an Uber and headed over to my birth mother's house here on Nantucket. Quinn is my birth mom. I live with her now."

Jessica wrapped her arms around the young girl. The girl didn't say so, but Jessica knew she needed a hug. "We both feel like orphans, huh?" Jessica asked the girl.

"No. I mean, I do, but I have to give Quinn a chance. I've been a great big pain in the ass for her, I know."

Just then, Andrew came down the stairs. He had his guitar, which told Jessica that he would be heading down to the beach to play his music, but it was early for that. He usually waited until the evening to go down to the beach and strum his guitar, because during the day, he was hard at work in his room composing.

He looked at Jessica, a hopeful note in his eyes, and Jessica went over to him. "I'm so sorry. I'm so sorry that I've been treating you the way I've been treating you."

He looked surprised that she was willing to speak to him. "That's okay."

"No it's not. No it's not. Listen, are you heading to the beach?"

"I am."

"It's almost time for me to take my lunch. I wondered if I could join you and tell you what's been going on with me?" Jessica asked hopefully. She was nervous because she would have to tell him that she was the one whose mother was killed saving his life. She was the young girl whose party he attended all those years ago.

She didn't know exactly why she was ready to talk to him about it, except for she knew that she was. Maybe it was because she finally cried for her mother. Maybe it was because she finally said out loud her mother was killed in front of her. Maybe it was because that young girl, with so much pain in her eyes, let her know she was not alone in grieving a lost parent. She realized she was not, by far, the only person who was dealing with severe trauma.

"Of course," Andrew said to her. "Of course. I've written so many songs since I last talked to you. I've been so anxious to get your feedback." His entire face was lit up like a Christmas tree.

She looked over at the young girl, who was still standing there with her violin in her hand.

"Thank you," Jessica said to her. "I didn't get your name?"

"Emerson. If you're working here, you're going to be seeing me. I play here every Friday and Saturday night with some dude named Deacon who plays the piano."

"Good to meet you Emerson," Jessica said. "I've been working here for the past couple of months. How come you haven't been playing all this time?"

"Quinn sent me to a nerd camp for other musical dudes. Just got back. It was pretty rad and I learned a lot."

"Well, I can't wait to hear you play."

At that, she and Andrew walked out the door to go down the steps that led to the beach.

It was the middle of the day and quite hot, it being July, and there were a ton of people in the water. The beach was crowded, but none of the other beachgoers paid Jessica and Andrew any mind, which was probably a relief to Andrew because he hated being recognized.

Andrew sat down on the beach and started to play, but then he stopped. "Before I start to play my music, maybe we need to talk. What's been going on with you?"

Jessica took a deep breath. " I know what happened to you when you were five years old. My mother was the one who threw herself in front of you. My mother was the one who saved your life."

Andrew's eyes got huge. "Oh my God. Your mother?"

"Yes. It was my mother."

Andrew put his hand over his chest. "I can't tell you how much guilt I've carried around for this. I've gone through so many hours in therapy because of it, and every therapist tells me it wasn't my fault, but I always feel like it is. And now I know it was your mother, and all I can say is how sorry I am. I'm so sorry."

"Andrew, you were five years old at the time. Of course, it wasn't your fault."

"I know. But I just have such survivor's guilt over the entire thing. My mother does too. She aged 20 years overnight after that incident. I remember that after it happened that she would just stare off into space for hours on end, talking to herself about why she would've married that man. And now, when we talk about it, she tells me she feels responsible for what happened. Just like I do."

Jessica took a look at the waves rolling in, one after another. It seemed there was a storm at sea that was rolling into the beach, and Jessica thought that that was appropriate for the situation – because she felt there was an internal storm buffeting her insides, again and again. The waves of confusion, sadness, and grief were what was filling the part of her missing all these years when she was not-so-blissfully unaware of how her mother had died. However, she was happy, at the same time, because she knew she could go through her grief. She could finally start to process it, when she never could before.

And she knew Andrew was going to be an important part of her healing. He was like the light shining through her broken pieces. She only hoped he felt the same way about her.

"You're not responsible. Your father was responsible, and maybe he wasn't really either. His mental illness, the war he was in, his inability to seek help when he really needed it was responsible. I'll admit, when I first found out what happened, I couldn't look at you. It was as if I saw my pain reflected in your eyes. I irrationally blamed you, much as you have been irrationally blaming yourself all these years. But it was not your fault. It wasn't your fault."

She looked at Andrew and saw that he was holding back tears. She could almost see the lump in his throat.

"Thank you for saying that," he said. "God, after it happened, I couldn't speak for three years. For three years, I didn't say a word. I wrote poems to express myself, but I never made a sound."

Jessica put her hand to heart when he said that. "That happened to me, too. I went mute, too, for two years." It seemed that that was yet another connection they had to one another - both of them were so traumatized it took both of their voices away. Literally.

And then he looked at her. "You. You used to go by a different name. Natalie. I've finally figured out how I knew you, why I was so connected to you. You were my first love, when I was only five years old. You were my best friend, and my soulmate."

Jessica closed her eyes. Somehow, this part of the story was not brought up for her when she accessed the memories of that day. But, she did sort of remember going by a different name when she was young. Well, actually, it wasn't really a different name. It was her middle name. Now that James mentioned it, she did remember that her father started calling her Jessica after she moved to California. After the incident. It was as if her father was trying to create for her a completely different life from the one she had there on Nantucket.

And, when she looked at James, she remembered him from all those years ago. Yes, he was her first love as well. Now, she remembered all those days at the beach with him. He never liked to get in the water, not like she did, but he liked to climb bluffs, throw balls, build sandcastles, and bury her up to her neck in the sand.

They were two peas in a pod the summer they met. They would hold hands as they walked along the shore, picking up sea glass, sand dollars and shells. He kissed her on the cheek, and she would kiss him back. She always thought he would be with her forever.

And that's why he was at her birthday party, of course. She had blocked all of this out of her brain. A part of her little girl brain knew her little friend was going through a tough time with his father at home. But, when you're that young, you don't really think about it.

"Yes. You're right. I used to go by the name Natalie, my middle name. Oh my God. I can't believe you're the little boy who I was in love with when I was only five years old. I have so many memories that were bottled up somewhere that featured you. Always you."

Andrew smiled and put his arm around her. "I have the same memories of you. I've been dreaming about you lately. Just about every night. Usually my dreams are of us at the beach, because that's what we did together. I have one dream a lot about you insisting your Barbies were going to live in my sand castle."

Jessica laughed. Now that he mentioned it, she could access those memories as well. "And you didn't want them to, because they were supposed to live in a big beautiful townhouse, right?"

"Right."

For the next few hours, Andrew and Jessica reminisced about the summer they spent together. Jessica really loved this conversation, because that summer was the last summer she was happy. Her mother was killed in September of that year. When the leaves were falling.

And that was the mother and daughter in her own visions. She now remembered she was wearing a red coat dress at her party, and her mother pushed her on the swing and she jumped off into a pile of leaves. That's the vision that she had all the time. And that was probably because that was the last good memory of her mother.

"So tell me what happened with your father."

Andrew took a breath, and he was shaking. "My mom was leaving him. I heard them fighting all the time. I would be in my room - my mother would always send me to my room when she knew there would be a fight. Sometimes when I would see her later on, she would have bruises on her arms. She would tell me she fell out of bed. I guess she didn't want to scare me. Anyhow, on the night before it happened, they had a vicious fight. My mother said she was going to leave, and he would never see me again. I guess he wanted to have custody of me, even though he had so many mental issues. And I don't know, I guess her threatening to leave made him crazy."

"How did he know where you guys were?"

"My mom told him where we were going that morning. I guess maybe she was trying to appease him a little. She told him that we were going to Codfish Park for a birthday party." He shook his head. "I want that day back so bad. In my mind's eye, when I relive it, something would've been different. Maybe my mom would've taken us to a shelter. Or maybe we could have just left without telling him where we were going. Even now, I wonder why my mother told him exactly where we were going to be."

"I know the feeling. I know what it's like to want to turn back time. Ever since I remembered what happened to my mother, I've been obsessed with similar thoughts. If only I was born on a different day. If only we would have just had a party at our house. A million and one scenarios have gone through my mind, all of them resulting in my mother never stepping foot in that park that day. But, at the same time, I guess it was just her time. If she wasn't killed by a bullet, she would've been hit by a bus. Her number was up, and there probably was nothing any of us could have done about it."

She remembered seeing the remake of the *Time Machine*. An inventor named Alexander invented a time machine so that he could save his fiancée after she was killed by a mugger. So he built the Time Machine, and he went back to the day his fiancée was killed by a mugger, and he changed what happened. He made sure she was nowhere near that mugger. She was still killed, but this time she was run over by a runaway horse and buggy.

Jessica knew that even if her mother was never near that park, she would still be killed somehow. That was just how it was with cruel fate.

She looked into Andrew's blue eyes and took a deep

breath. "I hope we can still be friends. I can't tell you how much I value being around you. When I met you, there was just something about you that was very healing. And right now, that's what I really need. To heal. I know you're going back to Los Angeles in a few weeks, but I hope we can still keep in touch."

He smiled. "You know, I can write music and compose it anywhere, really. I mean, obviously, I have to go to Los Angeles to record it, and then I'm going on a world tour to promote it. But I kinda like it here. Not so much traffic and you have room to breathe. I've actually been thinking about buying a house around here, a house by the ocean. I figure it's the best of both worlds. I can hop a plane to the studio and I don't have to deal with quite as much, shall we say, population density issues."

"Population density issues is a good way of putting it," Jessica said. She suddenly felt hopeful that maybe she and Andrew could still be friends even after he was scheduled to leave. She never thought they would be more than that. But that was okay. Just having Andrew in her life was enough.

"And you know, you're probably going to have to get some counseling about this. I want you to know that I have your back. Whatever you need, I'll be there," he said.

"Thank you so much. But I hope you're not saying that because you feel responsible, because you're not."

He shook his head. "No. It's just that I can relate to handling early childhood trauma, having done it myself for so long. I know what it's like to have PTSD, which is ironic, because that's what my father had when he did what he did. And I think you should probably look into the possibility of getting back into school. Like I like to channel my emotions into my music and poetry, you could maybe channel your emotions into getting back into school and scuba diving and doing all the things you loved to do."

Jessica didn't say anything. She still wasn't ready to face life. When she was working at the inn, it didn't feel like real life. It felt like she was just waiting to rejoin the world. Somehow, if she actually got back into school, it would seem like she was back to the real world. And that was scary as hell.

Besides, it took a lot of money to do what he was talking about doing. Money that she simply didn't have.

So, when he made the suggestion about her getting back into scuba diving, and probably surfing, and back into school, she just nodded her head. "Now, let's hear some of the new music you wanted me to hear."

He kind of cocked his head when she said that. He knew she was still running. And she knew he probably could understand why she would still be running. But, he didn't push. He just sang some songs, and Jessica closed her eyes and listened. And for those few hours when they were down on the beach together, she forgot everything.

And that was exactly what she was looking for.

CHAPTER 28

JESSICA

Two months later, around her birthday, Jessica felt like she was finally turning a corner in her emotions and her life. She had saved some money because she was living rent-free, and she was getting paid a small stipend on top of her room and board, so she didn't have any expenses. So she had saved enough money to buy some used scuba gear, as well as enough money to rent a boat for the day for herself and Andrew. Andrew had bought her a wetsuit as a birthday gift, so she gifted him two days on a boat. He was more than thrilled when she told him about the boat rental she got for them so that they could both go scuba diving over the weekend.

"I love it!" Andrew said when Jessica gave him the tickets she had bought for the chartered boat. "And what I love is that it seems you're ready to get back in the water, so that's a good sign."

Jessica nodded. "Yes. And the good thing about staying here with Ava and working for her is I don't have any expenses, so I'm able to save up money. After a year or so, I'm hoping I might have enough money to go back to school. I also need to hire a therapist to process my mother's memories and death. But I know I'm going to be able to do everything that I want to do, as long as I keep saving every penny."

But Jessica knew that her getting back into the water, scuba diving and surfing, were a kind of therapy for her. It was the beginning of her healing process and a significant part of it. Andrew's friendship with her was another crucial part of her healing, so it thrilled her to know that he was buying a house less than a mile away from Ava's home.

So, as she and Andrew toasted her birthday with her newly adopted family with a glass of fake champagne and plateful of delicious hors d'oeuvres, she counted her blessings. While she stood in front of the fire while listening to exquisite violin playing, she felt more peaceful than she had in a long time. She compared this birthday to the last and knew she was in a much better place this year than the year before. She was living here last year, too, but she was living here by herself, and she was addicted to OxyContin the previous year. Her family had shut her out, so she wasn't even welcome to spend her birthday with them last year. On her last birthday, she ate a hot dog and entertained herself by watching a marathon of old movies. It was a lonely birthday, and she felt nobody loved her, and nobody ever would again.

Now, this year, she had a new family. A family that was by choice, not by blood, and it was a family formed by caring and love. Ava was like the mother she missed all these years. She was much more of a mother to her than her stepmother ever was. She was more like the mother she had for the first five years of her life, the mother that was preserved in her memories but was not around for most of her life. She had also gotten very close to Quinn, Hallie and Sarah, and, of course, Andrew. She missed her father and her stepmother, and she regretted the fact that her actions drove them away from her. But she knew that having a family by choice was almost better than having a family by blood.

At least in this case, it was.

Made in the USA
Monee, IL
27 November 2022